And God Gives
Nuts To Those Who
Have No Teeth

And God Gives Nuts To Those Who Have No Teeth

HEINEMANN NEW WRITING

edited by

Heather Godwin

HEINEMANN : LONDON

William Heinemann Ltd
Michelin House, 81 Fulham Road, London SW3 6RB
LONDON   MELBOURNE   AUCKLAND

This collection first published in Great Britain 1990
This collection, together with the notes,
copyright © William Heinemann Ltd 1990
Reprinted 1990

A CIP catalogue record for this book
is available from the British Library
ISBN 0 434 82592 1

Printed and bound in Great Britain
by Clays Ltd, St Ives plc

This anthology has been compiled with the help of the Regional Arts Associations of Great Britain. My thanks go to them and to the many people who took the time and trouble to submit their stories.

Heather Godwin

Contents

A Day
at the Seaside

Linda Kempton

The children would be cross if they knew what I'd done. They won't find out of course. They mustn't. They'd be so cross. Especially Brenda. Brenda mustn't know of all people.

It'd have been all right if I'd been able to write. But I haven't. Not all week. Day after long and dreary day without writing. It's only the writing that keeps me sane. But this week he put his foot down. He knew I must be doing something I shouldn't because the house was in such a shocking state. He'd started noticing dust on the banister rails. And I'd given him a bought pie for his dinner. He said it was obvious my standards were slipping. A bought pie! His mother would turn in her grave. She wouldn't have had one in the house. And what was good enough for his mother was good enough for him.

I sat down and cried then. He hates it when I cry. Woman's weapon he always says. I say it's the only one I've got. Brenda never cries of course. Oh no. Not her. Even when she was a little girl she never cried. If you

3

smacked her she'd just look at you with that defiant look of hers. Challenging. Looking for a fight. Sometimes I really wanted to smack her. Smack her and smack her until she cried. But I never did. She's just like her father. The way she purses her mouth in that smug way of hers. And she's so irritating I could shake her. Always makes you feel in the wrong, feel stupid. Mind you I irritate her too. She says so. She says I've got an inferiority complex and that's a sign of weakness. Well she'd have been proud of me today all right. I was far from weak.

We woke at half past six this morning. We always do. Every night he sets the alarm for half past six. Come rain or shine. In all of my married life I've never slept later than half past six. Never once. Even when I was up in the night with the children I could never have a lie-in when they were sleeping. Lying in bed after half past six is slovenly he says. There's no need for it. People should go to bed at half past ten and get up at half past six. Routine and rhythm. That's what life's about. There'd be less crime and vandalism if only people would follow these simple rules. The devil makes work for idle hands he says.

'Come on girl. Half past six. Up we get.' And we get up. Just like that. No stretching or yawning or having a lazy five minutes. Oh no. Straight out of bed and into the bath. At least for me. He insists that I have a bath every day. It's more important for a woman he says. He has one once a week and he doesn't do much washing in between. It's the one thing that surprises me about him. The one thing that doesn't seem to fit. He's obsessive about me being clean and tidy, about the house being clean and tidy, but not about himself. I've never been able to fathom it.

While I'm in the bath he does his exercises in front of

the window. We're not overlooked. He makes all sorts of funny noises while he's doing them, but I've never been able to work out what they are. I think he thinks he's still in the army.

'Beautiful day girl. We'll go to the sea. Do us good, a spot of sea air. Tone up the lungs.'

Cheese and tomato sandwiches we had. We always have cheese and tomato sandwiches. When you've found perfection why change it he says. Routine and rhythm. Sometimes I've toyed with the idea of getting something different. Tuna fish perhaps. But I daren't. I'd never hear the last of it. When we first got married I used to try and make our meals varied and interesting. But he soon put a stop to that. There was no need for it. It was wasteful he said, although I've never been able to work out why. So now we have the same meal each day of the week. That's the way he likes it so that's the way it is. Roast on Sunday, shepherd's pie on Monday, liver on Tuesday . . . I could scream.

I have to map read for him in the car. It's silly because he's always planned out the route exactly before we go anywhere. I suppose he doesn't like to see me just sitting there. It makes me so nervous, map reading. I never could understand the things properly and I always hated geography at school. I don't know why it is, but it always takes me ages to spot things I'm looking for on a map, whereas he can see them straight away. I get so het up because he'll start making me feel a fool, with that exaggerated patience of his, as though he were talking to a child. Then he'll start to raise his voice and it'll end in tears. It always ends in tears.

There were some nice long roads today so I didn't have

to keep looking at the map. There was time to think. I was thinking about my writing. I've been doing it in the daytime and it's made a whole new life for me. I can put down on paper everything I feel. It's marvellous. I'm not very good of course. I just write a sort of diary, but it's more than that because I really let go with what I'm feeling inside. I'd like to try writing stories sometime, but I don't think I could.

It's funny how I started. There was this programme on the radio and it really made me want to have a go at it because English was my best subject at school. I'm not very good, but that doesn't seem to matter. I just love it.

Then he noticed that I was getting a bit behind with the housework. It's not surprising of course because the writing became a bit compulsive. I couldn't stop. So the housework began to suffer. Well he went up the wall. He wasn't going to go to work every day of his life just to keep an idle woman who didn't know the meaning of the word responsibility. So I've had to ration the writing. If I'm careful not to do more than two hours a day, I can keep everything spotless. Just as he likes it. Mind you I slipped a bit last week. I got carried away with this stream of consciousness thing I'd been experimenting with. I got a book out of the library about it. That's why he got a bought pie for his dinner.

I love the seaside. The day was perfect. Warm with a slight breeze that ruffled and lifted but didn't blow away. The sea smelled wonderful. Everything smelled wonderful. It was one of those days when each of your senses seems to be condensed inside your head, stronger and sharper than usual. I wanted to explode with joy. I remember I had to kneel down to tie my shoelace. My knee was bare and the asphalt under it was warm. I could smell it and feel it. So warm. I can remember when I was a little girl, I was always kneeling on the pavement or in the road, playing. It took me right back. You're so in touch with everything then; everything's so real and immediate. Your senses are so aware. I tried to tell him about it but he just looked at me as if I were a fool.

We walked along the beach. I had to take my shoes off. I can't bear the feel of sand in my shoes. It makes me want to scream. Like having my nails cut too short.

There was a Punch and Judy show. He spotted it before I did. He loves anything like that; anything slapstick and childish. I just hate slapstick and I'm no longer a child. But I did love the tent. Oh yes. That was straight from a picture book. Orange and yellow stripes it had. And the curtain had scalloped edges. But ugly, horrible Punch with his hooked nose and demented screaming, he always makes me want to shudder. 'Judy, Judy, Judy.' But he stood rooted to the spot, mouth wide open and laughing uproariously at the stupid thing. He looked ridiculous in his shirt and tie and tweed jacket. He hadn't even taken off his shoes and the sand was spilling over the tops of them, slipping and sliding all over his feet. The children's laughter was beautiful though; high and sweet and unforced. What a contrast.

The breeze lifted the corner of the tent slightly. I watched it lifting and falling, brushing the sand. And then a sudden gusting lifted it higher and it slapped back down with a sound like a pistol shot. The sun was warm on my back and the moment was trapped as though all time had stood still. The tent; corner lifting gently. And the warmth, just touched by the breeze. And the children with their open mouths and wide eyes; they hadn't noticed anything of what was really happening. Only the raucous screeching of those ridiculous puppets.

He decided that we should find somewhere secluded for our picnic. Heaven knows why. We'd nothing to talk about. Nothing to say to each other. I wanted to stay and watch the children and the donkeys. I wanted to watch real people having real conversations. But no.

We headed off for the cliffs, driving along the coast road. He always drives very cautiously; too cautiously. People are always overtaking him, with their fists shaking or horns blaring. He's a menace on the road really. He shouldn't be allowed.

We managed to find somewhere very quiet. Isolated. It was a lovely spot, although there were signs telling you to be careful because the cliffs were eroding. Such a shame. I wonder if they can stop it?

We sat on the tartan rug, quite close to the cliff edge and so high that I felt as though we were on the edge of the world. It made me feel a bit giddy. I've never been too keen on heights.

We didn't say very much. But one of the advantages of not talking is that you're free to think your own thoughts in peace. I have to make sure that my face is fairly composed though and doesn't look too relaxed, otherwise he asks me what I'm thinking about. And I never know what to say. Today I thought about a poem by Betjeman, 'Trebetherick' I think it's called. Sand in the sandwiches, wasps in the tea. There weren't any wasps today though. I'd have loved to have just sat there, reading it. But that would have been out of the question. He can't abide poetry. Self-indulgent rubbish he calls it. In fact he doesn't like me reading at all. We haven't any books in the house. I have to hide my library book under the mattress. I don't know what would happen if he ever found it. He doesn't like to see a woman with idle hands. I can't just sit down in the evenings and watch television. Oh no. He wouldn't tolerate that. I have to keep my hands busy, have some knitting or sewing to do. But I'd love just to sit there and read sometimes.

Out of the corner of my eye I was watching him eating. I always do. I don't know why. I suppose it must be a form of masochism. I get so angry. His thin little mouth pursed up, so precise, so prissy, going round and round. Routine and rhythm. Routine and rhythm. Chewing each piece seventeen times, just like his mother told him. Today he had a piece of cheese in his moustache that moved up and down as he chewed. And his nose was red and shiny in the sun.

After we'd eaten he said he'd go for a stroll. So after I'd cleared away the picnic things I was able to sit for a while. I watched him walk away, stiff-shouldered. Stroll's the wrong word of course. He could never stroll. Strolling suggests relaxation. He never relaxes.

When he was out of sight I lay on my front, just looking out to sea and enjoying the peace. I must have dozed off because I remember that he was suddenly standing on the cliff edge with his back to me. The gulls were wheeling and diving and clamouring. It was fascinating the way he was standing so close to the edge. I would never have dared.

When I stood behind him I could see the diamond pattern on the back of his neck, the criss-cross lines of elderly men. The silver-grey hair above them was too short and stubbly. I could see the white scalp through the bristles. But it seemed all of a piece somehow; with that

9

back, straight as a ramrod. When I put my hands on his back I could feel the rough tweed, warm under my fingers. He turned his head over his shoulder, startled. And I saw the pink skin and hairy ears and pale eyelashes. But he couldn't stop me. He was too late. I felt so strong when I pushed, although I was surprised at how little effort it took. I laughed for joy and freedom and power as his body sailed through the air. The gulls seemed to swoop with him at first, but they were able to pull out of the dive of course. His body was so graceful as it fell. I was rather proud of him. And of myself. In fact the whole world seemed to applaud. The sun sparkled on the sea, the breeze lifted my hair and the gulls continued their squawking and diving.

I was proud of myself afterwards too. The police were very kind and I was rather amused underneath as I watched myself playing the distraught widow. There'll have to be an inquest of course. But the erosion's very bad just round the headland. It could have happened to anyone. I expect they'll fence it off now.

Oh well, I suppose I ought to tear this up. I should be in trouble if anyone found it, and I don't want that. Not now that my life's just beginning. And of course Brenda mustn't see it. Not Brenda. She'd be so cross.

Special Strength

Alan Mahar

I

You'll be wanting an explanation. I'll take it slow. Talking's not my strong point. As you know. Except with a few cans of S.S. inside me. But I'm not dumb. Just because I work with my hands doesn't mean I can't write things out. There are questions I'd like to ask you. If I ever get to see you. I can tell you some more about the decision I came to. You were clever though. Or was it coincidence? I only recall that the night before he appeared I was walking you home.

I'm walking her to a taxi office because outside it's not safe for everyone. Buses are a thing of the past. She hasn't got a vehicle herself. And sometimes I choose not to drive mine round the city. When I get the chance at night I chase the lights, stay awake a few hours longer. There are others who do the same. I've seen them.

Just as she's stooping into a Toyota Corolla, perfume and cushions, Mahmood her usual driver, she says innocently: *Why do you have to work nights?* I'm shagged out and I don't have to hide it with her. She touches my leather coatsleeve with her hand. *Couldn't you drop the nights?* I took it as a compliment. I enjoyed our time together too. *It's only every so often.*

I go over everything she said.

2

I have a season ticket for the swimming therapy. Courtesy of the Corporation. Hardly anyone else goes when I go. Except half-cripples. Nobody really talks to anyone else. And women have to go on different days. I stay under the water for a long time. Hold my breath for 75 seconds; I've practised. That's supposed to help the skin. The Baths Company is the only quiet place I can bear.

I first met her there. She checked the tickets and watched for accidents. Attendants are trained to inspect the skin at the small shower by the entrance. My patch is no more than itchy. She looks for livid signs. She told me not to hold my breath underwater too long. *Bad for your heart.* She said her father taught her confidence in the water. *Trained me himself the different strokes.* Lucky then, I said. *And he took me walking along the river that wiggles between the factories, showed me balsam and rosebay willowherb.* Not so fortunate, I said. *Then he died on me. Heart-busted with the early-retirement option.* All when I first met her.

I've seen the old men in the baths with their bloodless legs and all the grey veins showing. As soon as they hit water they're fish, ancient carp that understand the reason for their slowness and a long life. The water separates for them, and then zips back up when they take their leg kick up the bath, following the lines of the cracks in the tiles.

Sunlight through the glass in the roof improves their appearance. I don't talk to them ever.

I thought I saw him there once, just above the stable door of one of the cubicles. He was towelling his eyes before he put his spectacles back on. Wet calf lick across his brow. He manages to stay younger. Some of them can. They have special interests and spend all day on the exercise machines, while the rest of us work. They haven't had to for a few years. But that's a minority that know what to do apart from clean away their scraps of rubbish. Dead time for most of them. I have the chance to work extra and I wouldn't think of refusing it.

3

The size of this building though, that's something, and only me inside. An enormous box encasing great space and volume: all the waste at the centre of the processing plant. High walls without rooms, without floors. I sort through the rubble mounds, move mountains to the incinerator shaft. The grabber travels easy on a gantry above the expanse of the pit. Thick breeze block walls, no windows: straight lines and rectangles. High white smoke stack adjoining. Geometrical forms. We send the smoke over. Who knows in the night where it gets wafted?

I've never had a fear of heights. Surgical mask protects from the dust. White hard hat for cranium safety. Lager to sluice the throat. The stench that wafts up from below can even be sweet for a moment before it is nauseating. The rubbish. The convoys of container trucks unloading round the clock.

I've got the cab fitted out comfortable for all the long

shifts. Four-packs of *Special Strength*: it doesn't alter my concentration. Headset playing trumpet high and loud. Freddie Hubbard. 'First Light'. I shake my head. Do the shout inside. With me it's the fast thing. Noises pinging in the brain.

What do I think about when I'm up there? Shapes. Lines. Parabolas. Swings. Angles. Distances. Nothing else. I'm guessing and gauging every pick-up and every drop. They pay me decent money for a good eye. I like being high up, and then dropping the grabber arms, opening them at just the moment, cupping them around the object. Then I trapeze it gently over the chasm. Right onto the spot. It's a point of honour. I don't drop things. Not accidentally.

4

I can talk to her because with her I don't stammer. She didn't try to finish my sentences. Gave me time. I don't lose track of them at all. The ideas rattle out like trumpet fire. Speech always the impediment. Except in my apartment we can blather on in noughts and noughts about distances and planets. *You CAN talk when you're not half-pissed*, she says. When we talk. When a meeting is arranged. We sit at the window. 14th floor. No need for curtains so high up. We can lie around naked on the bed after a good fuck and look out. I put my music on. Trumpet time. She sits, hugs her knees. I'm not sure she hears it the same. We watch the winking lights on flight paths. The worming trails of tail lights on motorways. Stars, planets, satellites. The drink works on me. Patterns I have chased on electronic games. Colours, lines. Everybody's reflexes need to be good.

And what about this planet that we're on now? The Rainbows would say there's some danger. I listen. In the next flat I can hear a vacuum cleaner going. I couldn't say I keep a tidy place. I've never seen my neighbours, but I know they're old, the way they mutter and clean.

She tries something else. *You see, anyone can go in the Baths Company. All the pestering old men I meet – not even a man with interests. Well, except I met you didn't I?* I jump tracks on the CD, don't like the slow ones. *But the Environment Corporation is a different matter, isn't it? That whole area by the railway fenced off and patrolled. Creepy, if you ask me.* I listen to her observations. I want to lick her hips instead. I say: *It's not interesting to talk about. I transfer garbage in enormous volume. Same every day.* She pulls away from me. *Okay,* I say, *have you any idea of the tonnage I shift every day?* I tell her some more astronomical noughts. She laughs. *See. No wonder I get a bonus.* I offer her one thickish bicep to press. *Strength, stamina. That's why I get the special night job. Simple.* I stroke her leg skin: hardly a mark. My touch doesn't quieten her.

Might that have anything to do with the big marshalling yards? Heavy rail movements, large freight in the night. I have to be careful. *Could be. I don't know from one week to the next. I just do the loading. No fuss. That's it.* They don't give me details about the really special loads do they? Nobody even says the N-word any more. They're hardly likely to give me the train timetables in advance. Simple security. I just get a phone call. And I don't talk about it. Even after a drink. They've tested me. *I don't ask.* All I know is lifting special loads requires special care. My eye, my hand, my strength. I see the official danger logos on the side of the bulk carriers. I know what it is. *Why are you so interested anyway?*

I'm just trying to get you to talk. The stammer starts up then.

5

He was pleased whenever I took a girlfriend home. Then he would talk affably about his garden herbs, and collect dandelion leaves and spinach for his salad bowl. *Salads don't have to be so predictable*. Then he'd use his infuriating modesty: *We can but try*. We drank his ginger beer and sipped his nettle wine. He discoursed on their properties and invited the girl in question on one of our Sunday walks. He would ask her if she had an interest in hedge-rows. I lost different girls either mild October or sunshine May. He charmed them all with information, learning worn lightly. And I still stammered. They always lost touch nicely though.

In the garden he worshipped at his compost heap. He liked to see the grass cuttings cause it to steam. Vegetable leaves in a separate boxed area, weeds always bagged separately, and secured with green twine for the dustbin collection. If it was operating; sometimes the Corporation deploys staff elsewhere, and people try to complain about no collection. He took a pleasure in keeping a tidy garden, dutifully packed the waste bags into the van for the civic amenity. He never failed to sharpen his spade and his hoe after every Saturday 'tilling'. He wore a beret and Swiss walking boots. At one time he had an allotment he marched to; something was built over it – a garden supermarket.

Not the necessary curiosity for a scientist, I'm afraid. Never once picked up on the interests I put your way. Accused me of failing my exams on purpose. *Some childish revenge, is it? How could geometry be enough on its own?* That was an ancient battle. I wish it didn't matter. It doesn't. We could have come to blows. I developed a capacity for lager. In his collector's collection the record racks of steam engines, birdsong, Shakespeare formed one part of a whole wall – all the classical symphonies and the history of jazz. Young Armstrong, yes; I don't hate all the old. Otherwise I only ever listened to Clifford Brown's supple trumpeting. None of his other records was of interest to me. I discovered the video game arcades: Star Wars, Intergalactica, SDI, Missile Attack. I spent some money. Still do when I can find them. Test my speed.

6

I'd even forgotten that I'd been in this city before. Once I could operate a crane, every site seemed much the same, every Portakabin, every cab a home from home. The arguments, the brew-ups of tea, the little rolled-up newspaper passed round.

Don't imagine it was anything but the money brought me here. Not a question of coming back home. A section of a district of a region. That's all. A venue on a worksheet. Next year I'll be somewhere else. North Coast B. Somewhere with spoiled beaches. No I don't have any special feeling for this city. I memorise afresh the roads, the lights, the railway lines. And they're the same and different anywhere. But I'm privileged inside the Corporation complex: I can look down the railway line, past each bridge, all the way to the skyscrapers; and I'm not appalled by the waste space on either side. I only hear of the clearances there have been, and new uses for emptiness. The steam railway museum's another scrapyard, the BMX track redundant: no one can remember children ever being interested. Cleared space makes the view simpler. The railway leads to the city; these towers to those towers; the dilapidation located there and the dormitories somewhere else.

I had to travel away for the work. A disagreement over exams. My future. No qualifications. We couldn't be under the same roof, the two of us. Then the long wait in rented rooms for the chance of an HGV licence. Transport, warehousing, construction – I tried them all. Something about Environmental I found conducive: the shifting of massive weight; the special crunch of sizeable materials; good riddance to bad rubbish; no one wanting to talk. Don't ask me what. I showed an aptitude. I was quick; I was accurate at judging distances; I was available for work; and I kept my mouth shut. They ask me; I always say Yes.

It was a special job. A train coming through the Midlands. A dangerous load has to travel slowly between power stations, and none of the protest people has to know. From South Coast C up to North West A. Our plant conveniently half way between. I move the load from one train to another train waiting. Perfectly safe. The waste processing plant is conveniently next to the marshalling yard. So I go from long hours on the waste disposal – that's my usual; then this extra work with the trains. In someone else's cab. But I take my four-packs to feel at home: my *Special Strength*. Nights, of course. Some loads have to be under cover of darkness. Floodlights to work in. Special care. I'm not frightened.

7

So when I see this Mitsubishi van pull into what used to be the public area, the civic amenity, I don't suspect anything. There's nothing different. Someone's tipping garbage, like they did before the checkpoints and the intercoms. I forget about the change in public access.

It could be wood in a pile, garden sods in fertiliser bags, crowswing umbrellas, the polystyrene squares for videos and computers. It might be beer cans and ring pulls, pop bottles and tangles of audio tape. Yoghurt pots and chip papers, burger packs and catfood tins, shiny foil freezer meal trays and Embassy packets full of ash, dried tealeaves in eggshell halves, sodden balls of Kleenex, all toppling out of heavy duty black bags. This is how it happens every day. I don't mind it myself. It gets tidied away. The grabber sorts it. Out of sight and up the chimney.

I'm in the cab and I'm looking down. I see the usual shape on the VDU, one of our chaps shifting something. Then I freeze-frame on the figure bending to unload the van, remember again the Corporation ruling cancelling the civic amenity. I don't know what made me look closer. The studied walk, the quiet confidence. And the flash of grey hair under the beret.

Woodshavings, privet clippings, wallpaper strippings, and sump oil flagons, perished bricks and splintered guttering. Smashed glass TV sets, opened-up video recorders, typewriters, transistor circuits, vacuum cleaner bags spilling. The sparrows always at the new mounds, checking. I didn't see him coming. I'd forgotten. It wasn't in my mind that he lived here. He would have had a way of getting past the barriers. He could always talk people round. Security guards in booths, middle-aged pensioners in bifocals. He's one of those that waved the old survey maps at farmers. The politest of troublemakers.

8

She started asking again about this extra responsibility. I say I keep the headset whirring; I crack open the cans. Don't give it a thought. Was I at risk from these campaigners? she wondered. Rainbows had broken fences, left messages inside. But my skin hasn't got any worse. Anyway I trust the security force at Environmental Corporation. They'd know what to do with cranks. *I expect they're what you call nice people. The worst sort.*

She wants to contest my flippancy immediately, of course. She thinks I can't mean it. *I know lots of nice people who don't share your views. A whole group.* She was speaking of her allegiances more than she meant to. I should have guessed then, but I didn't. *An old man I know, he talks to me sometimes about wild flowers and garden vegetables after group meetings. I mean, no one knows that stuff any more. I love to listen to his quiet voice. He's not trying to prove anything.* She's been taken in by all that pretended weakness. Words that insinuate a power over you. *Well, I've met his sort before. Quite deceptive really.* Her gullibility was a disappointment to me; or else she was clever and needling me. Either way I sensed us reaching conflict. *I like him. The old ones are not all the same. He wears this curious beret.*

9

I lift him up so he can see me in the cab. Face to face. See how he likes it. See if he realises. All that time struggling. I draw him up level with me. So he can see me. Recognise me? Long time. Now everything could be equal, more or less. He could be made to understand. But I'd no idea what I'd do. Something just so he knew. I drop him down. I let him fall. Out of the grabber arms. He tumbles in, a dust cloud rises. He's trudging in the shifting matter. He's struggling for a foothold. I'm watching. I finger the cab controls. I'm counting. Holding my breath 75 seconds. Watched the sparrows gathering a safe distance from commotion. On the headset a fruity trumpet blast from Freddie Hubbard speaks up against sentences too sensible. There. An easing through noise.

I'm able to look down again: the man was speechless, pleading something. Perfectly powerless. I swing the grabber down to him. Speedy levers open out the hand for him, close round him, pick him up and deposit him on the parapet. He's back by his van brushing dust off his boots, pulling at his beret. One look up at my cab. That's all. He climbed into his van then.

10

I don't really want the Corporation to know who he was. It could go down as an accident, couldn't it. It was: he shouldn't have been there. They don't need to know.

I didn't find out till later, he collapsed on his way out. Trying to drive away. Wedged into his steering wheel at traffic lights. Face all contorted from the attack, the security guard said. I saw a Rainbow sticker on the back window of the abandoned Mitsubishi.

Why would I connect him with you? Couldn't we meet again? I might understand more of your questions. You weren't using me to find things out were you? I can tell you I've given up the night work now. Finally. I did give it some thought, see.

Every evening I've been to the hospital. Now I have a chair at my father's bedside. He can't talk the way he used to. Not yet. I study the blinking of the electrocardiograph. A new light for me to follow in the night. I find I am gripping his hand with all my strength.

Real Raspberry Jam

Sue Sully

Down among the raspberries I remember a childhood summer. The smell rises up through the leaves. My grandparents' garden. The dark kitchen. The smell of boiling jam.

I can see James waving at me from the sitting room window to let me know he is home. I gather the last handful of raspberries from beneath the leaves and make my way slowly to the house.

He buries his face in my dry hair. I know where he has been. I can smell her perfume on his clothes.

'You smell of raspberries,' he says.

'I'll wash them in a minute. We'll eat them without cream. Just sugar. The way you like them.' My voice is too anxious to please. I know that I have irritated him.

'You could make jam,' he says. 'Why do you buy that nasty artificial stuff from the supermarket when you could make it?'

I feel myself stiffen. I pull away from him and he stands with an exasperated smile, his arms spread, as if to say, 'Now what have I done?'

I say in a silly bright voice, 'I've never been a jam-maker. You know that.' And as I begin to wash the raspberries at the sink I hear him walk away from me.

I can still picture the frayed rugs on the floor, the scrubbed deal table and the black cast-iron stove. My grandfather, swinging the small suitcase up from the floor. 'Let's have that off you. Front bedroom is it, Mother?' He smiled at my grandmother as though asking permission to move.

My grandmother nodded. She put an arm round my shoulders, but when he had gone she let it fall and went to the dresser drawer. She spread a brown oiled cover on the table, on top of that a stiff white cloth, and in the middle she set a plastic jam pot holder which held a jar of raspberry jam. She stood, as if admiring the exact placing of the jam at the centre of the table, then, remembering me, she took a box of cutlery from the drawer. 'Best make yourself useful.' She said it kindly, but as I set out the knives and spoons my heart beat in my throat, with fear that I should get it wrong.

'We're in for a treat, our Kath.' My grandfather pulled his chair up to the table. 'First pot of the season.'

'You'll not eat it all at once,' my grandmother warned, but there was a pride in her voice, and a secret satisfaction which pulled at the corners of her mouth.

'Do you hear that?' He turned to me with a fierce stare. 'No spreading it in great dollops all over your bread and butter, or we'll have to send you back a week early and tell your mum and dad you're eating us out of house and home.'

He winked. My throat, which had tightened at the rebuke, relaxed with a strange, embarrassing burst of laughter, and I giggled for longer than was necessary.

The bread lay in soft white triangles on the plate. The jam, red as stained glass in a church window, fell liquid from the spoon.

'Enjoying that, are you, Kathleen?' my grandmother said. I saw that she was smiling at me. She could not have been old then, but she seemed so to me. Her hair, drawn back from pale cheeks, was rolled into a bun behind her head. She always wore an apron, which had tiny flowers on it and bulged like a pillow above her waist. And she wore a silver brooch, a pair of lovebirds on a sprig of blossom, which clasped the collar of her frock up close about her neck. She always looked the same. She hardly ever smiled, but when she did, it was like a ripple moving through very still water. She never held me without there was a certain formality in the embrace, and I would remain stiff-limbed against the flowered apron, sensing her reserve. And yet I loved her, and I felt her love for me. Not in her touch, but when one of those rare smiles came my way.

'There's nothing so downright honest as a pot of home-made jam.' My grandfather's garden-grimed fingers worked the table-knife across his bread, spreading a bright wound on its surface. He said, 'Who wants that artificial and nasty shop effort, after they've sampled your grandma's jam?'

My grandmother looked at him strangely then, a swift, knowing look, which brought a colour to her pale cheeks and made him shift his eyes away.

'Why is shop jam artificial and nasty?' I asked. My mother always had shop-bought jam at home. It tasted like real jam. No one had ever suggested a nastiness about it before.

'Some people like that sort of thing,' my grandmother

said, and there was a harshness in her voice which struck a fresh chord of anxiety in me.

My grandfather was silent. Then he smiled, an artificial smile, glossy, bright. 'Well now – ' He was looking at me, not at my grandmother, and with that same fixed smile on his face. 'Have I ever told you about the time my mate Tommy Clarke and me went round the back of the jam factory, to see if it was true they put wood chips in the jam, to make it look like it's got real raspberries in it?'

I shook my head, dumb with picturing it.

'Tommy and me went round the back one lunchtime, and there they were, great barrels lined up in rows. You could see inside, little chips of wood, like sawdust, our Kath. Waiting to be added to all those jars of shop jam and stick in the gullet of some poor unsuspecting customer.'

'I know what sticks in my gullet,' my grandmother said with sudden venom. 'And it's not raspberry seeds.' She patted my hand with a quick soothing gesture, for she must have seen my stricken face. 'There, don't upset yourself. It's only one of your grandad's silly tales.'

'It's true as I sit here.' He folded his stubby fingers over his waistcoat, and for a moment I hated him. He was a large man with a heavy face, which my mother used to call handsome. He had a moustache which was always stained with tobacco. There was pink now from the raspberry jam among the ginger bristles.

'If you're a good girl,' he said, 'your grandma will show you how to make real jam one day.' He leaned forward and pinched my cheek, and I could smell the tobacco on his hands. 'A lass should know how to make jam. Get you a husband one day, that sort of thing.'

★

It did not attract me, not the making of it. The rows of empty jars and the sugar in thick blue paper bags lined up on the table, the flip, flip of sound from the pan on the stove, and steam which filled the gloomy kitchen with the smell of boiling jam.

But the raspberries were different, hanging like soft, dark pink sweets among the leaves at the end of the garden.

There was a path at the end of my grandparents' garden. It wound behind the raspberry canes, to peter out among weeds and nettles by the compost heap. Here I made a den, tunnelled into a patch of long grass close up against the fence. Here, in the days which followed, I traced the veins of raspberry leaves, pulled squeaking grass stems from their sheaths to suck the pale, bitter stalks, watched beetles scale grassy peaks and climb boulders as I trapped them with my hands. Here, with the drifting smell of raspberries, I stayed, dreaming long hours, until dusk fell with its sudden shiver, and the midges itched, and it was time for bed.

At night I lay in the little front bedroom which smelled of lino, under-bed-sheets stiff and musty from the chest of drawers. I listened to my grandparents in the room below. Their voices seemed to come from a long way off. They rose and fell, my grandfather's heavy, my grandmother's stabbing with shrill bursts of anger. They merged, parted, hovered between sudden silences, and began again. Once, there was a longer silence. I heard the slam of the front door. I thought I heard my grandmother crying. I drew the sheets up over my head to shut out the sound, and I rubbed my midge bites until they hurt.

★

My grandfather was getting ready to go to the row of shops at the end of the street. I watched him brush his hair smooth and straighten his tie in the hall mirror.

My grandmother had been picking raspberries. She was dragging the jam pan from the kitchen cupboard. I could see the tops of her stockings when she bent down, thick and brown and fastened with suspenders, and her white thighs like slabs of lard. She straightened. 'You'd better take Kathleen,' she said. 'She can spend her pocket money.' She brushed a strand of hair away from her eyes, and the look in them which she fixed on my grandfather was cold as chips of stone.

I walked beside him on the pavement, not wanting to accept the offer of his large dry hand when we crossed the road. I felt the scratchiness of his tweed jacket against my bare arm.

'What are you going to buy with your pocket money?' He gave my hand a squeeze. 'On what are you going to squander all your worldly wealth?'

I replied awkwardly that I didn't know.

'Don't know?' he said. 'Don't know? A long perusal is in order then, before the glorious squander.' He laughed, as though he had said something funny, though I didn't know what the words meant. He seemed distant then. He dropped my hand and began to whistle something, a tune I had heard on the wireless. The music he made was clever and cold and thin.

When we reached the shops he said, 'I want you to be a good girl and look in the window a few minutes, Kath, while I go into the newsagent's and fetch a paper.' He was smoothing down his hair, looking at his reflection in the window.

'Can't I come with you?' I whined. 'They've got *The Topper* and *The Beano*.'

He looked annoyed. I twisted my plastic purse in my hands and snapped its metal fastening. At last he clacked his tongue against his teeth and nodded, and I followed him inside.

The shop was empty except for a woman behind the counter. I buried myself in a corner, next to the rows of comics. I jingled the coins in my purse and read the picture stories on the comic covers, while my grandfather talked to the woman in the shop.

'So, that's the little granddaughter, is it?' I heard her say.

I lost interest in them then and concentrated on Biffo the Bear. Biffo's football had been stolen by a bully who had kicked the ball into a tree. I drew in my breath at the caption, which pointed to a wasps' nest among the tree branches. I had been stung by a wasp once, the previous summer.

The woman asked my grandfather a question.

'Making jam. What else but?' I heard him say.

The woman laughed, and murmured something I couldn't hear.

'You're not the domesticated kind,' my grandfather said.

I looked at them. He was leaning across the shop counter, and the woman laughed again, a low crooning sound. She was smiling at my grandfather with her eyes very wide, she had red lips and long black hair.

I stared hard at Biffo the Bear. The bully was running away. A cloud of dots trailed a long 'Bzzzz-z' after him. My grandfather was talking again quietly, as if he didn't want me to hear. He used a word which I had never heard a grown-up say before, one of the less familiar adult words of which children sometimes boasted a knowledge in the playground, I only half understood it, though I knew that it was dirty. My grandfather repeated the word, soft and coaxing, like someone talking to a cat.

'Lovely *nipples*. Nipples like raspberries, that's what.'

She giggled. 'Shush, Joe – the child.'

I took *The Beano* from the stand and walked with it across the shop. The woman pulled her frock tidy at the waist and gave my grandfather a warning look. He turned with that bright false smile which closed my heart against him.

'Now then, our Kath. Have you chosen something?'

'I'd like this comic, please,' I said in a cold, grown-up voice. I looked away from the yellowed moustache. I stared at his fingers spread upon the counter, the nails edged with black, and broken at the ends.

'So, this is the little granddaughter,' the woman said again.

'Goes home to her mum and dad this afternoon. Isn't that right, our Kath?'

I did not answer. I held out my hand with a sixpence in it. I thanked the woman politely when she handed me the change.

'She's a serious little soul,' my grandfather said. 'Takes after her grandmother, I shouldn't be surprised.'

I did not speak to him all the way home, though he tried to joke about this and that. He was jaunty now, with his newspaper tucked under his arm, and his other hand holding mine. He swung my arm up and down every now and then. But I could not forgive him for that word.

★

They did not hear me later when I went into the kitchen. My grandmother was stirring jam with a wooden spoon. My grandfather stood behind her, he was talking to her quietly against her ear, his hand was cupped round the bulge of her flowered apron and he stroked one of her breasts slowly with his thumb.

I stared at the two of them, his hand on her breast, and him crooning into her ear, like when he had talked to the woman in the shop. My grandmother's work-reddened fingers held the spoon against the edge of the pan. She stood very still. It was then that I saw that she was crying.

I sought my den behind the raspberry canes. I hid there in the long grass, with the sour smell of the compost heap, and the brush of stinging nettles against my knees.

Some time after that, we must have had raspberry jam for tea at home, because I remember repeating my grandfather's story about the barrels of wood chips outside the jam factory.

My father laughed. He said that it was just one of my grandfather's terrible pub yarns. He said that people did not deceive other people like that. But I would not eat the jam. And, as I looked at the small, wood-pale seeds pressed against the side of the jar and the red brilliance through the glass, I began to cry and would not be consoled.

I brush away the tears with one hand, and coat the raspberries for James with sugar. I ladle spoon after spoon over them, the way he likes them. I vowed a long time ago that I would never make jam.

The Triumph
of Jessie Jones

Daphne Glazer

Shortly after Bert had died in the lav, Jessie had had to be carted off to the loony-bin. She just couldn't think what to do next. Bert had always told her what to do. Barbara and Wendy and Eddie had come to see her.

'Mam, you've got to get better quick – brought you a box of "Black Magic" – just to cheer you up!'

They'd talked to her in special voices. Eddie had even shouted and she'd rounded on him. 'Eh, lad, I might be daft but I'm not deaf.'

She'd sat there after they'd driven off in Eddie's 'Avenger' and had gazed at the ladies and gentlemen shuffling about in their carpet slippers or staring vacantly before them.

Suddenly on an afternoon in early March when the sun was shining and she could see snowdrops growing in clusters under the trees in the hospital grounds, it had occurred to her that she was just like the other inmates . . . somehow she hadn't thought of it that way before. They were bloody irritating, she had to say it. A woman called

Mildred would keep asking her what time it was. One bloke groaned all the time and there was Rosie who wouldn't stop popping her dentures in and out. Added to all that everything seemed to smell of boiled cabbage and gravy. She'd felt like giving a few sharp blasts on a nice lily of the valley fresh air spray. Basically though it was Rosie's dentures which settled it. She lost them and accused Jessie of pinching them, and they were finally discovered under Jessie's pillow. That was when Jessie decided she was better.

On arrival back at her terraced house she'd looked around with something of a shock. The nets shone whiter than white, the table and sideboard gleamed and there was a gentle aroma of lavender polish. A card saying 'Welcome Home' stood on the mantelpiece. Every sign of Bert had been removed – no caps, cigarette packets, jackets, shoes had been left. They were saving her.

'Shall you be all right, Mam?' Babs had enquired, earnestly. 'Don't want you getting upset again, do we?'

'We've just had a spring-clean, like – the lasses that is,' Eddie had grinned. He was like his Dad, a joker – couldn't stand anything to do with cremis or cancer. He dismissed weepy things by saying they were 'morbid'.

'Yes, love,' she'd said, 'was very nice of you all . . .'

They offered to take her to bingo, for treats at the fish and chip restaurant, and then, as summer was coming on, for day trips to Brid or Scarbro.

'Must get you out, Mam.'

People had been saying that for years. Even Bert had offered occasionally to take her to the club, but she'd always refused – she'd been 'Mam', 'our lass', who stayed

at home and looked after three kids and then the grand-
kids. Mam had nerves, that was a known fact.

Bert in one of his sharp suits would be slapping lavender
hair oil on, standing in front of the mirror and humming
'I'll be loving you eternally' or 'When Irish eyes are
smiling', and she'd be wondering what he did down there
every night and what Irish eyes were smiling at him. He'd
been a docker, a bull of a man with a red face, a lined
forehead and blue eyes like sapphire chips. He'd not been
above laying into her after one of his boozy 'do's' – but that
had been early on in the marriage.

One brilliant summer's day she was in the yard pegging
out sheets and pillow cases when she saw Edna from next
door leaning on the fence and looking across.

'Eh up,' Edna shouted, 'I've heard there's a nice little
job looking after toilets.'

Jessie went on pegging, but she listened.

'Why don't you have a try for it, it'ud be just up your
street?'

Edna had recently been divorced and was working part-
time in a newsagent's, selling cigarettes and sweets.

'You need to get out, love – dun't do to stop in so much.'

'Oh I don't suppose I could really.'

But Jessie thought of Rosie's dentures and the smell of
boiled cabbage and she screwed up her courage and the
following morning, without telling anybody, she put on her
best pale blue mac, took her shopping-bag, and set off for
the job centre in town.

She got the job, mainly because she looked too grim to
allow customers to slip into the lavs free of charge, also she
had the scrupulous cleanliness of the determined cleaner.

'Start on Monday.'

'Start on Monday,' she was terrified. Her heart fluttered and she wondered whether Bert's heart had done the same when it was giving out. Well, she consoled herself, at least if you were dead, you didn't have to bother about it.

'I've got it,' she announced to Edna when they met later at the fence.

'Geraway!'

'I have . . . but I don't know whether . . .'

'Now, love, what you need is a new look . . . image, you know. You must do something with that hair.'

'Yes,' Jessie said, thinking about Rosie's suet-grey face and dusty grey hair through which the dingy white scalp had shone. 'Yes . . . but what?'

At the hands of Debbie at the 'Rhapsody Salon' Jessie underwent a transformation. She emerged as a dizzy, strawberry blonde with a bubble perm. All the way home she kept peeking at herself in shop windows. This new person amazed her. Her mind began to run on exotic outfits . . . she who for years had worn shapeless 'Courtelle' 'reach-me-downs' and navy-blue or bottle-green polyester skirts. She felt sure an attack of 'nerves' would come on and she waited for the onset of her palpitations and breathlessness . . . but it didn't come. Yes, she promised herself, with her first wage-packet she would buy a new creation.

On Monday morning after a weekend of feeling dizzy and nervous, Jessie started her new job.

'It might be too much for you, Mam,' Babs had said. 'You don't *have* to do it . . .'

They all thought she was a patient . . . she remembered their special voices and that was when she knew, she would be going . . . even if she dropped dead in her lavs, she was going.

Her domain was down by the pier, where the ferries used to chug across to New Holland. She'd once made the trip with Bert and the kids. Bert had spent the voyage drinking bitter in the bar, while she'd followed Babs, Wendy and Eddie round, making sure they didn't plop into the water. It had been both exciting and sick-making. What would happen if the ferry sank? She'd read the instructions about life-belts . . . oh, it had been like a journey to the end of the earth.

As she entered the handsome brick building with its heavy oak doors which were fastened back with curly brass hooks, she caught a whiff of that day. Her memories were mostly about averting accidents and placating Bert.

The floor was marble . . . lovely white-veined slabs, the lavs had oak doors and their cisterns bore the name 'Dreadnaught'. All the doorknobs and even the hinges on the lavatory seats were brass . . . she would make them shine.

In no time she was mopping that floor, working her mop among the white detergent peaks in her bucket and then swirling it across the smooth expanse. The marble came up brilliantly and she paused to admire it.

The customers came in a steady dribble, young girls with bare legs, teetering on spindle-heeled shoes, women with babies, juggling bags and pushchairs. She offered to hold the babies while the mothers entered the oak portals. Then there were ladies of her own age murmuring about the heat and their legs and the weight of their shopping bags and the way it cost 5p in old money for a wee-wee . . . and why should women have to pay when men went free?

Somewhere in the middle of the day, she found herself singing – it was a quite extraordinary thing. It began as a dull rumble, not unlike the start of a flushing cistern, and then it took off.

'When Irish eyes are smilin' . . .' and 'I'll take you home again Kathleen to where your heart shall feel no pain . . .'

The words merged with the soft wash leather stroking the coloured glass in the door of the booth, which was her little rest-room; the place where the cleaning things were stored. There was an electric kettle for her use.

At 1 p.m. she took a break and sat on a green-painted wooden seat near the lavatory and looked away across the heavy cord-grey estuary to the horizon, where phantom ships dithered in a heat haze. Somewhere in the muddle of her uneasiness a certain comfort was spreading . . . she hardly knew what it was, because it was so unfamiliar to her. She was a woman who had spent a lot of her life being afraid.

At the end of the first week she bought a black cotton sweater threaded with Lurex.

'You should see me Mam,' Jessie heard Wendy muttering to Babs, and got the idea that she disapproved. They thought she was bonkers. Jessie felt a laugh urging up her throat and she sneezed.

After several months, one day when Jessie was giving 'I'll walk with God' all she'd got and rubbing madly at the brass plates on the lav doors, a voice interrupted her.

Jessie had just reached, 'From this day forth . . .'

'Eh, love, you ought to be doing the clubs with a voice like that . . .'

She was being addressed by a blonde lady with bunchy

scarlet lips and azure eyelids who was gleaming like the angel Gabriel in a white cotton trouser suit.

'Clubs!'

'Yes, love – you'd really go down like a bomb there.'

Jessie blinked and blushed and paused.

'Listen, I'm Mrs Mallard – you come down to the "Green Dragon" on Saturday – eightish – and I'll introduce you round.'

It was a matter for an urgent chat over a cuppa in Edna's kitchen. Edna's advice was, 'Saturday, you're on!'

And so the two women, Edna in a white pencil-slim skirt and white jacket and Jessie in a silver Lurex top and black trousers, sat very upright in the back of a taxi.

'This is it, love!' Edna whispered, patting her blow-waved hair.

Jessie had spent an hour getting ready, smoothing on layers of tropical pancake and darkening her eyelashes and eye-brows with mascara. Terror alternated with excitement. Perhaps she really had gone loopy! And they were going in a taxi too!

'I feel like Lady Muck!' she giggled. Edna allowed herself a smile. She felt as wobbly as though she'd been the one to sing.

There was a little stage at the 'Green Dragon' and a microphone. Jessie saw it and quailed. She felt she was certain to have a bad turn.

'Edna, I can't do it,' she whispered to her friend. 'I'm bloody finished.' She had a sudden vision of Bert turning on her, as he had done so often, particularly in the early days – later she'd given up anyway – 'You . . . you couldn't do owt like that . . . never . . .' when she'd wanted to have

a part-time job as a barmaid. Yes, it had always been . . .
'You . . . what, you!'

'Here, get this down you!' Edna slid a big brown drink towards Jessie who took a deep swallow of it. She thought of her son's incredulous expression as he'd met them on the door-step when they were just about to board the taxi.

'Mam . . . what's this?'

'Singing,' she'd said, trying to sound light. Yes, he did think she was bloody bonkers.

'That gentleman over there's bought you another.'

'Oh, thank you!' Jessie gave a fond beam and despatched that drink too.

'Give us a song, then!' they were calling. This was it, the moment she'd never expected, never dreamed of. As it was happening, she was aware both of its dreadfulness and of its thrill. She thought her heart would burst. Up she got and she tottered out onto the platform, feeling how her new winkle-pickers dug into the corns on her little toes. Never mind.

Now she was standing before the microphone. The faces swam below her at the tables. She was launched, her voice throbbing strangely in her throat . . . '"If you ever go across the sea to Ireland . . ."' It's all right, she thought, all right. She heard the hotness in her voice and she began to love it. All at once the hands were smacking together and the rings and glasses sparkled.

"Core, encore . . . core!" they bellowed. They didn't know what they were glimpsing in that funny bundle of a woman whose voice gushed out like something that had been imprisoned for an age . . . at first it was tentative and then brash with life.

She did two more. They were banging the tables and stamping their feet.

When she sat down, drinks appeared as though by magic.

'Eh, Jessie, I was real choked hearing you like that!' Edna said. Tears were tracking her bronze cheeks.

Later, travelling back home in the taxi with Edna, Jessie still heard the drumming of the feet and the clashing of hands. I'm blotto, she thought, and at the same time the words eased into her head – I'm me . . . yes, I'm me . . . I'm not the bairns and I'm not him . . . I'm me.

Orchards

William Bedford

Every night the fox came down from the hills and hid among the trees. You could see its traces in the summer grass, hear the vixen crying on heat. With the first snows, delicate footprints appeared between the rows of trees, and there were scuffles in the mud at the edge of the stream. On the trees, dark patches of fungus discoloured the infected bark, and where the canker had spread, whole branches were rotten with disease, causing fruit spurs and buds to wilt and shrivel near the scab. There had been no apples that year, and the trees looked pathetic and sick, the dying wood creaking when the fox cried in the night.

Lowther was certain it was the fox damaging his trees.

'What else can it be?' he glared aggressively when the men in the pub said he was imagining things. 'You tell me what else it can be?' He kept their gaze, his eyes sullen with drink, his fists clenched round his glass. The older men were wary of him, knowing his temper, some of them remembering his father. The younger ones were not so sure.

'You spray for weevil and caterpillar?' one of them asked.

Lowther glowered into his empty glass.

'Bad year for sawfly,' another grinned, enjoying the joke. They all knew what was wrong with the trees. 'You want BHC for that,' the man said innocently. 'So I heard say.'

'Malathion,' his friend corrected.

'That's red spider, mate.'

'And sawfly.'

They were beginning to argue, enjoying themselves, when Lowther suddenly interrupted.

'I'm telling you, it's a fox,' he said viciously, glaring round at the men. 'It's a fox.'

'Course it is, mate.'

Lowther staggered up and fastened his coat. He stank of drink. He hadn't shaved for several days and his stubble was flecked with grey. As he leant against the table, the older men finished their drinks, waiting for him to go.

The man who had talked about sawfly stared at the fire.

'Summer pruning,' he said insolently, not bothered about Lowther. 'Could allus be that.'

Lowther watched him indifferently. His eyes were red from lack of sleep. The skin underneath his eyes was bruised with tiredness. For a moment, he looked surprised, glancing at the younger man, then his eyes clouded over and went blank. He drained his glass and put it down carelessly in front of the man.

'Goodnight,' he said with a sneering humour. As he pushed past the table, he slipped against the wall, and the men moved nervously, one or two of them beginning to laugh. He laughed with them, raising his hand. He felt dizzy. By the time he reached the door his head was spinning. 'Goodnight,' he shouted again, slamming the pub door.

The ground was iron with frost. A cold wind moaned up the narrow lane and the snow was packed like ice, solid in the rough road. Near the hedges, where the snow had drifted, it was frozen a foot thick.

'Bastards,' he said, shivering against the cold. 'Bastards.'

Far away, he thought he could hear the fox crying.

The Lowthers had always owned the orchard at the far end of the village. Ignoring all advice, the father had planted the original trees in soil that was too heavy for them, on a rough bit of ground exposed to cold east winds. The stream at the bottom of the orchard made the earth marshy and damp. Everybody knew James Grieve was a daft tree for this far north. It was prone to apple scab and canker, and the fruit was liable to bruise. The best late variety would have been Orleans Reinette, or maybe even Golden Noble, not this pale yellow fruit with its flush of soft red streaks. The old man insisted on planting what he wanted, saying he preferred something with a good juicy flavour even if it was rotten. He planted the wrong trees out of cussedness, and left the orchard for his son who went on trying to crop the apples.

Lowther sat in the kitchen and warmed his hands at the fire. He boiled a kettle and heaped coals onto the range. He massaged his aching wrist, rheumatic from an old bit of damage. When the kettle boiled, he made a drink of hot water laced with cider vinegar and honey, and shuddered at the bitter taste. He laughed, staring into the flames. On the scuttle and brass fender, the light of the flames danced and shimmered. Holding up his glass, he could see the melting honey, yellow in the warm light.

He remembered his father, scything the huge orchard.

Vigorous, and in a rage, the old man flailed at the weeds, cursing the wild garlic and bluebells, the purple bell-flowers that had seeded from the hedge, the dandelions that were everywhere. The ditches were rampant with cow parsley and nettles, the grass at the sides of the lane humming with flies and bees. In a temper, the old man bent the scythe into the ground, wrenching his back and yelling with pain and frustration. He shouted at his son to buy a weedkiller, but Lowther refused, laughing, good-humoured. He spent all day spraying acres of crops with pesticides, and wouldn't see them used in the orchard. They fought over the trees, arguing about storing the rotten fruit, disagreeing about the wild flowers. Blind with fury, the old man died the year Lowther got married, and was buried in the church grave-yard, his tombstone now smothered with yellow lichen.

The sharp cry of the fox was like a cough in the blistering cold, threatening, intermittent. Getting up from the fire, he stood uneasily by his chair. He was confused, listening for the cry. The flames were burning low. He threw more coal on the fire and then wondered why he didn't go to bed. On the mantelpiece stood the old army photograph of his father. He had never thrown it out, not noticing, indifferent. The fox cried again. He opened the kitchen door and the wind moaned into his face. The sky was full of stars. He blinked, flinching from the cold, and closed the door. There was no point going out. He sat down and stared into the fire, finishing the drink for his arthritis.

He knew why the orchard was dying.

She had wanted it kept natural. On her first visit, they

walked together beneath the shading trees. She worked in the town, travelling every day on the bus. In the new council houses, there was no room for proper gardens, and her parents weren't interested. She listened to him naming the flowers. At their feet, the grass was thick with snow-drops, drifts of wild hyacinth blue beneath the cloudless sky. They lay down in the warm grass and gazed through the clouds of blossom. In the middle of the orchard, primrose and yellow loosestrife caught the sun, pale in the shimmering dazzle. Down by the stream, forget-me-nots danced in the shallow water, marigolds and ragged-robin shone yellow and pink in the brilliant sun. When they came back to the orchard at night, the air was heavy with the scent of wild garlic, the sickly-smelling meadow-sweet which grew in great masses along the stream. She made him go into the water for forget-me-nots, and laughed softly when he took off his clothes to dry.

'You do what you want,' she whispered when the old man went on about the weeds. 'Don't listen to him.'

The afternoon they were married, she made him lie down with her in the orchard and make love in the sweet-smelling grass, the old man watching from his bedroom.

Then she started complaining. She hated the journey into town. The house was too far from her parents. She took a job at the pub, helping most lunchtimes and some evenings. When the regular barmaid left, she asked if she could have the job full-time. She came home too tired to speak, working late at night, getting back when Lowther was already asleep. Slovenly, bad-tempered, she lounged round the garden wearing tight jeans and an old blouse. One morning, when Lowther was getting ready to work in the orchard, she pressed him back against the kitchen table with a helpless groan, her hands hot and clumsy in her fumbling haste. A week later, she went off with another man, taking all Lowther's money from the post office and leaving the back door wide open in her hurry.

That was last year, when the air was dense with pollen, the country heavy and breathless with vegetation. Even the churches, built of the local greenstone, sank back into the lush growth. Old walls were covered with thick green moss. Gardens were overgrown with hollyhocks and sunflowers, great banks of lilies and roses clambering out of control.

Drunk with the scent, drowning himself in alcohol, Lowther savaged the trees in the orchard, his hands blistered from hacking at the vulnerable bark, his head aching with the silence and immense heat. All morning he went at the summer pruning, and collapsed in the afternoon weeping in the dry grass. At night, in his bedroom, he lay and listened to the hedgehogs, foaming in their frenzy on the lawn.

He did no spraying at all that year, forgetting the winter-wash and the bud-burst spray he was supposed to do the following March. At petal-fall, he couldn't be bothered with sawfly and spider mite, and the caterpillars were everywhere. He should have cut the diseased wood out with a knife, cleaning the wounds and painting them with a fungicidal paint. The branches that were infected should have been lopped off below the wound. By the time he noticed the damage he had done, it was too late. The trees were alive with woolly aphis, the apples were full of larvae. Dark patches appeared all over the bark. The fruit dropped rotten from the branches.

Stunned, he sat in his kitchen and listened every night to the fox.

It was coming down from the hills to find water in the fast-running stream.

On summer mornings, he would find its tracks baked in the hot mud.

Its stink seemed to hang over the stream.

The fox was suddenly at the edge of the orchard.

Looking up, Lowther flinched from the abrupt noise. The ragged harsh barking coughed on the low wind. Judging from the sound, it was now crossing the field beyond the orchard, nosing towards the water of the stream. The water was frozen solid.

Nervously, Lowther stood up.

'I can hear you,' he said angrily, tensing as if he was listening to the wind, his dulled nerves aching.

There was a scuffle in the hard snow in the garden.

'I can hear you,' he shouted to the blinds, the curtained windows.

This was ridiculous.

Without thinking, he unlocked the door.

The wind tugged at his hair. He felt his face freeze, his eyes flinch from the cold. He shut the door behind him and stared at the empty garden. The cold bruised his hands. When he breathed, the air made his throat ache. Over the fields, the sky was desolate with stars, a brilliant, hard moonlight. He could hear the snow creaking, freezing in the gutters and drains. The watertub was inches thick with ice, great overhangs of snow frozen in the metal gutters.

The fox cried down by the water.

He could take his gun but that would mean going back

into the house. He glanced towards the warm light, and then plunged into the frozen snow. He was still wearing his boots, though his coat was hanging in the kitchen cupboard. He ploughed through the snow, climbing the low fence into the orchard. In the moonlight, everything was bright and exaggerated. He could hear the trees, moving slowly in the cold. Every branch stood out, black against the pure snow. When he knocked into one of the trees, he was showered with falling snow, cascading from the low branches. He shook his head, the snow running down his back, freezing his bare shoulders. In the middle of the orchard, the ground was treacherous with ice, slippery where falls of snow had scattered. He fell awk-wardly, grazing the skin on his arm, jarring his knee against a tree trunk. His hands and face had gone numb, and he could hear the blood pounding in his ears, like a voice whispering in the shadows.

It took him several minutes to reach the stream.

The fox was waiting by the water.

It watched him for several seconds, and then pawed indifferently at the ground, scraping at the solid ice before turning and trotting across the field. There were scuff marks all over the ice. Fresh snow at the edge of the field had been churned and dirtied. In the moonlight, the fox ambled through the snow, and then darted under a hedge and back towards the hills. As it went, he heard a sharp cry, and then an owl flew low over the orchard, a weasel screamed its terrifying squeal.

He broke the ice with the steel caps of his boots.

It took several hard kicks, and then his leg plunged into freezing water, soaking his trousers and making his head reel with shock. He dragged his foot out of the water and stood shivering on the banks. With another kick, he shattered the frozen surface, and then turned and walked back through the orchard.

Big Beryl

Wilma Murray

I met her first at lunchtime on a sunny Monday in August. Beryl does not like Mondays, especially sunny Mondays, which is why she is on the roundabout, the one that cost the Council £43,000 back in the early seventies, excluding, that is, the cost of a thousand daffodil bulbs which were planted later. The roundabout is one of Beryl's special places. I am informed of this at once.

'Hey! Bugger off! This is my place.'

I stare. She is sitting on a checked rug among the sapling birch trees on the carefully landscaped hump. She has a picnic laid out in front of her, a picnic that would have done Queen Victoria and John Brown proud.

'Did you hear what I said?'

'Look, I'm sorry. I didn't see you.'

'What are you doing here, anyway?'

'It's my car. It's . . . Why am I explaining this to you? This is a public place.'

'Yes, but it's my public place. Now, piddle off.'

I sit down at a decent distance and try not to study her,

for she is a heavyweight, all rolls of soft fat, like a large blubbery seal. She catches me looking at her.

'I eat. What do you do? Play with yourself?'

I laugh, embarrassed. 'You have a sweet line in conversation, lady.'

'Want a sandwich?'

'No thank you.'

'What's your name?'

'John. What's yours?'

'Beryl. Hi, John.'

'Hi, Beryl.'

She continues her picnic. I stand up to look out for the AA. I realise then that the hollow in the roundabout where we are is entirely hidden from the roads which feed into it. It is a totally private place among all the traffic. I know then why she has chosen to have her picnic here.

'Do you come here often?' I say it and then laugh, realising.

She grins. It is an open, honest grin. She has a fine face.

'Only on sunny Mondays.' She does not explain.

'Where do you go on wet Tuedays?'

'The Reptile House.'

She juggles with more of my questions, then I must leave. I shout back to her on the way down. 'See you some other sunny Monday?'

'Suit yourself.'

Crazy woman. Yet I catch myself thinking about her at odd moments during the week. I want to laugh, remembering. The next Monday is cold and drizzly, but the one after is fine. I pack a modest picnic. I am surprised by my eagerness for a second encounter.

She is already there, on the checked rug, eating.

64

'Hi. Remember me?'

'How's your antique Mini, then?'

I am absurdly pleased to find out she watched me that first day. 'Recovered. Want a sandwich?'

'What's in it?'

'Tuna. Lettuce.'

'Yuck.'

We eat in what silence is left to us below the noise of traffic. We move a step nearer to the pattern that begins to emerge out of the random mosaic of our days. I learn much about Beryl.

I learn that the children she teaches are the only truly honest commentators on her condition. For that, she loves them. I begin to sense something of her self-inflicted isolation. Only, she calls it freedom and I do not understand. We speak of many things, of books and work and we set the world to rights on sunny Mondays on the roundabout.

'Why do you go on doing this to yourself, Beryl?' I have to ask.

'Do you care?'

'I care.'

'It's easier this way, believe me. I've made my choice and I've learned to handle the flak.'

I chuckle. 'I've noticed.' I look around and feel I have more to share with her than the sky. 'Couldn't we go somewhere else next week?'

'Like?'

'Oh, I don't know . . . The beach?'

'People.'

'I see.'

'No, you don't.' She picks up a large peach and bites on

it. The juice dribbles down her chin and drips on to her
smock. I watch till the peach is gone, seeing her complete
dedication to the enjoyment of it. I begin to feel a kind of
anger. Anger and shame.

'I'm not house-trained, you see,' she says.

Suddenly I wish myself anywhere but on this roundabout; in a crowd, with normal people, anonymous.

'You couldn't handle it, could you?'

'No.' I admit it.

'Well, in that case, get the hell off my roundabout.
What's the matter with you, anyway? Why aren't you off
screwing some skinny bird somewhere and boasting to your
mates about it?'

I pack up my things roughly and retreat with relief.

'I knew you were a prawn!' she shouts after me.

I am hurt and angry, as though I've been bitten by a pet
dog. Fat cow! I avoid the roundabout for many Mondays,
sunny or otherwise.

But I do see her again on a wet Tuesday in the Reptile
House. I sit on the next bench. I do not speak, just stare at
the lizards. She and they stare into space. She is not eating,
but there is a picnic spread out beside her. Suddenly, a
lizard darts across its cage, tipping the careful balance of
the mood between us.

I speak first. 'What have you been doing with yourself,
then?'

'Oh, just trundling along in the self-destruct mode, as
usual. Practising suicide notes.'

I am startled. 'You're not . . . ?'

She laughs at me. 'Oh, no. I tried that once. Too messy.
Never did get the dried sick out of my shoes properly.' She
looks at me directly for the first time since I sat down. 'Oh,

and don't flatter yourself. It was a long time ago.'

I grin inwardly. I can feel the comfortable, easy lightness return to my gut.

'You're some woman. You know that?'

'I won't change,' she says, at last.

'So?'

'So why don't you just piddle off again and save us both a lot of hassle?'

I ride the tide of her gloriously familiar aggression, grinning.

'Want a sandwich?' She pushes the box to the end of her bench.

'What's in it?'

'White Stilton and pickled gherkin.'

'Yuck.' I take one, anyway.

Torch

Steve Garner

I was in prison when I saw her. She was on the local news. When I got out I hired a Vauxhall Viva and spent five days watching her house. On the fifth day she came out. I drove up alongside her and wound the window down. I said, Can you tell me the way to – ? Then I grabbed her wrist and twisted it hard. I said, Get in and no funny business, there's a gun in the glove compartment. It was a starting pistol but she wasn't to know that.

I drove her to the house. It stood alone at the end of a track where people left their rubbish. There were boards at the windows. I shoved her into the kitchen and locked the door. There were no lights in the house, only candles, and the walls were running with damp.

I kept her there for two weeks. Sometimes I fed her in the morning, sometimes at the dead of night. Once I woke her up five times in one night to give her the same meal, baked beans cold from a tin, and dry bread. After that I didn't feed her for three days. I brought in a Chinese and ate it in front of her eyes, and when I saw her looking at me I snapped my teeth. This was to disorientate her, to make her lose all sense of time and place. I wanted her to be totally dependent on me. I wanted me to be her god.

At the end of the two weeks I shone a torch into her face and said, Show me how you do it. She said, Don't make me do that. I said, You won't eat until you do. I blindfolded her and tied her into her chair. In the next room I built an altar to my god. I placed a green onyx dish on the table and surrounded it with all the things I'd stolen, lighters and books of matches and a tin of petrol. I found an old telephone directory and set it alight. The flames licked the shoddy pages and turned yellow and blue, whispering. I held it as long as I could and dropped it into the wastepaper basket when the god bit my flesh. It turned black and dropped apart. It struck me that I had destroyed a whole town. I was sweating and fulfilled.

I woke with the breath of the god in my skin and my hair. I spent the rest of that day in perfect peace, meditating. I read books about unexplained phenomena; spontaneous combustion and the fire walkers of India, who can cross glowing coals barefoot by thinking them as cold as ice. I read Shakespeare, the death of Portia in Julius Caesar. And, because the hour of my triumph was so near, I permitted myself the luxury of thinking about myself. I'd been inside for setting fire to a chemist's that sold a certain brand of aftershave. It was supposed to make you irresistible to models. They had no trouble in resisting me, in fact they gave me a very wide berth. The psychiatrist said I'd a chip on my shoulder. I disagreed with him. That's no chip, I told him, it's sinew and bone, it's a bloody great hump. You can touch it if you want to know what I have to drag through life. He wouldn't though. His name was Dr Emm. That's not a real name.

I thought about the first time I had discovered the god. I was playing, alone as usual because I was a freak; I had stolen some matches and I was bored. I could hear the shouts of the other kids from the park; it was a still July evening and they were playing cricket. I set fire to some bushes, I watched them burn and I heard the voice of the god in the flames, telling me to go out and burn things, all the things that people save all their lives for, all the trash you see in shops, the Schreiber wardrobes and the mock Tudor cabinets, the things you can get on HP on easy terms, the fantastic bargains, the shit. I stared at the flames, the bright colours, I wanted to be in the heart of them where it was black. I forgot my hump and my ugliness. I took off my shirt and got as close as I dared. My chest went red and I was running with sweat. The god had kissed me and I was ecstatic and afraid.

I knew I was not alone. The god was a jealous god, he wouldn't let me share my secret. I had no one to share it with anyway. I kept my pockets filled with lighters and boxes of matches, they banged against my leg when I walked, on the inside. That made me feel restless and strange but it felt good. I never knew when the god would speak or what he would order me to burn: a pile of rags in a garage, an abandoned car. I was his slave but even that was power. It was like walking through a crowd of imbecile faces and knowing that you had a knife in the pocket of your coat, and that you could turn round at any moment and carve their smug grinning cheeks and no one knows this but yourself. I kept things under my bed, I was always secretive but now I grew more so in the god's service: tins of paraffin and lighters I stole from shops, bits of charred paper I held up to my lips and kissed and kissed again, marvelling at the smell. Things gave me hot secret joy that fools could not guess at: the smoothness of a match with its red tip full of power that could destroy a whole town, a candle with wax dripping. I told none of this to that idiot trick cyclist.

About the girl? I was perfectly confident. After three days in the chair she was willing to do anything. I said, Show me, then. She said, Don't make me do it, don't ask. She said, Tell me what – and I pointed to a rag on the floor. She stared at it and nothing happened at first. I was shaking with impatience and rage. I would have to kill her, slit her throat and bury her under the nettles at the back of the house. She had caused me nothing but trouble, I thought.

Then a thin jet of smoke spurted from the rag and it caught alight. I whirled and skipped round the kitchen, I howled and sang and stamped the fire out and put the rag to my lips. I nuzzled it and tasted the charred breath of the god on my lips. Come on, I said to her. We're going for a little walk.

I got the handcuffs out and slipped them over our wrists. Tell me the secret, I said. I thought that she could teach me the art and I'd dispose of her later. She wept and said she didn't know. If she thought of something long enough it caught alight. Her parents had thrown her out twice, she'd caused untold amounts of damage. A priest had tried to exorcise her. Everyone hated her, and she had no friends. Just like me, I thought, another freak. I can't allow myself to think, she said. Her voice was slow and slurred. I supposed that came from sitting motionless all day, and not allowing yourself to think.

It was three in the afternoon. We went for a walk round the shopping precinct. I told her to concentrate on things: a paper in a man's hand, a walking stick, the ridiculous fake books you see in certain furniture stores. When these things went up in flames I roared at the fear and consternation it caused, the drooling amazement, the dervish prancing, the flapping hands. But these were mere pranks. I got photographs for her, new swimming baths and a town hall in Basingstoke that had won some kind of award because it didn't have any windows. She concentrated over them and next day we heard they'd been burned to the ground.

Her range was thirty miles. Once, with an hour's concentration, she managed to destroy a conference centre in Aberdeen. She said the night was unusually still and her thoughts were like wireless waves. I was elated. I'd suffered for my god but he had rewarded me, I could burn the whole world and reduce it to ash. I wanted to travel, like death. I wanted to raze the Vatican and Buckingham Palace.

I thought it best to move on, even though no one was looking for her. I didn't bother disguising her sallow skin and coarse features, the ugly hands. We moved twenty miles south, to a town the same as the one we'd left. We rented a very brown room and I got a job delivering leaflets. If you ordered ten pizzas you got another one free. Like an abortion on a plate. One afternoon I came home, to find her standing by the window, watching the lorries. I asked her what was wrong. I love you, she said.

She was crying and twisting something round and round

in her hands, it was a sock I'd taken off the night before. It wasn't particularly clean. I went into the bedroom and contemplated this love thing. I hadn't expected it. I had no reason to be smug about my effect on women, indeed, I always knew what it would be in advance. But she was a freak like me, I supposed that had done it. I hadn't foreseen this. I paced the brown linoleum, thinking, an ecstasy of indecision. Finally I decided it would be all right. If she loved me I could have her dancing attendance on my every scowl, walking on tiptoe and wondering what she'd said or done wrong. It was another form of revenge. I remembered the hours she'd spent in that kitchen, the hard times I'd given her, the times I'd blindfolded her or bound her wrists and ankles with cord, the Chinese burns. It was logical enough. I'd cared enough about her existence to inflict pain. And she loved me because of that.

She worked hard at being in love. I watched her. She folded my shirts and kissed them, she put things away in drawers. I patrolled the Legoland estates and stuffed leaflets through doors, I attended meetings where I got told that the way to Nirvana was through pizzas and everyone must play his part. Sometimes I burned the leaflets. But I was thinking more and more about her, I started to miss her when I was away, we were two freaks and we were made for each other, we had gone through the same insults and taunts, the patronising questions, the beatings. I'd never been loved before. The fire, the god, demanded love but it never gave it back: that family I lived with in Wales had seen I'd been clothed and fed but if I'd have burned myself to death in one of my early experiments they'd have 'phoned up and got another one, like a budgerigar. She held me as if she was frightened of letting me go, as if she wanted to burrow through my flesh to the twisted spine that was the root of my being and thoughts. I lost my power, I fell in love. One day I came home with a chipped plate I'd bought from a stall, something to put in a drawer. I forgot my hatred, I forgot my allegiance.

I fell in love with her. Was that so wrong? Your body is straight and you have children and an attractive wife, and a house that is full of things – would your god really be so offended at the sight of two freaks in love? I didn't want the things, I couldn't see the sense in getting married, and as for attractive, well, that was a joke. But I couldn't exactly pick and choose, she was all I could get and that was more than I had had before in my life. I forgot the fire and the hatred inside. We didn't burn anything for weeks. It was stupid and mad, I was getting above myself. I almost thought we were normal, at times.

I was out one afternoon when I had one of my panic attacks. I hadn't had one in years, not since before I went inside. Something like a huge hammer hit me in the chest, it swung down from the sky and disappeared and when I looked up the sky was everywhere, empty and vast, it was a great dome and something was pressing down on it from above, some monster that wanted to break through and crush me like an egg. The streets were too wide, the universe wanted to suck me in. I dropped my bag and started running in my peculiar way, back to the house. I suddenly felt that something strange and terrifying was going on back there, I half expected to see a monster on the roof. What I was most afraid of was her being dead.

I ran up the stairs and found her crying in the brown room. I put my arms around her and Dearest, I whispered, what's wrong? In the early days of what people would call

our relationship endearments stuck to my palate like mush.
But now I found I could use them quite freely, throw them
around with gay abandon in lieu of full stops. That just
shows how bad things had become.

She said she wanted a baby. I'm sick of being a freak,
she said. The words thrilled me. I saw a child running
through some park, there was sunlight and trees and it was
a girl-child, it wore little white socks and a pink dress. I've
no time for boys, I remembered them in the playground,
jabbing my hump with dividers. I wanted to create instead
of destroying, I wanted our love to make things. We were
playing at being normal, we forgot what brought us
together, and the name of the god we were born to serve.
We wanted to be like everyone else. That's rich, isn't it?
That's the biggest joke of all. I want to scream and howl
with laughter now I think of how I felt, I want to lie on my
back, on my ridiculous hump and kick my legs in the air, I
want to snort and bellow until tears run down my cheeks.

She said, I know how it's done. She went into the other
room – it wasn't a room really, just a curtain to hide the
bed – it was what they called a studio flat, meaning a cesspit
ensuite, with brown lineleum and walls. I stood by the
window, smoking a cigarette. That should tell you how far
I'd gone in my madness. In the old days I didn't smoke, I
thought it was sacrilege, turning the god into a pet. But I'd
changed. I'd forgotten my god, and now I was due to be
punished, in the midst of my happiness. My heart was
filled with love. I wanted to do things for her, I wanted to
write a sonnet. But they didn't teach us things like that at
school, they said we'd be bored. We learned how to mend
sewing machines instead.

I put my cigarette out and went behind the curtain and

lay down next to her. That was the first time I noticed that
her eyes were beautiful. I lay on top of her and I saw the
child hanging in the red cave of her belly, waiting for me
to give it life. I fed it everything and its mouth opened and
cried for more, I saw a hand no bigger than my finger
opening and tugging on the black, I saw pink toes unfurl
like tiny banners and scrabble for a foothold on life. My
woman gurgled and rocked and gave little cries. Then her
scream changed, it became higher and continued climbing
until it wasn't there. I was listening to the child, its mouth
was open and black, it wanted everything, the room and
the bed and the chair, it wanted all of me in order to live.
A great wave broke in me and I gave it all I had, the prison
with its smells of hopelessness and piss, the kids throwing
my satchel about, the smell of fear and the burning grass,
the shops filled with bargains, the white hotels with no
room for me. I rode along the very edge of the wave, the
white foam, and it cast me up on a damp shore and I
opened my eyes. My hump was lying beside me, on the wet
sand.

I looked down at the woman I loved and I was terrified.
Her eyes were filled with pain and her mouth prised itself
open, she wanted to tell me something but it was too late.
There was a flash of pain across my belly like sheet
lightning, and I moved. I stood watching as her front
started glowing white, I could see her insides, her liver and
heart and for a second the child I had made. It was
screaming. Then the explosion came and I covered my
face. When I looked again there was nothing, just some
tubes on the bed that popped and coiled and smoked and
went out.

I sat on the floor and howled. I cursed the god for paying

me back in this way, I moved my enormous head from side to side and bellowed. When I stopped crying it was morning and the foul little room was suffused with grey light. I picked my hump off the floor and screwed it back on, tighter and heavier than before. Its weight was almost too much to balance, my legs buckled on the stairs. I slammed the front door and carried on walking, carrying my hump to the station.

Killing the President

Patrick Lambe

The two men struggled across the desk, locked in each other's grip, each tasting the salt of bitten lips, anticipating the bite of the knife they so desperately shared.

The older man, the President, thought, this will not kill me, this boy, this child, this young man who could be my nephew, my son – I am grey iron, I have sinews like veined rock, I have ancestors, wealth, power. But his grip quivered, and the knife hand slipped a fraction closer to the President's throat.

Until the desk was surrounded by men, holding and beating a thrashing, wild-eyed figure, knife obscure and forgotten under the desk, the President panting and brushing his suit, trying to remember the fierce breathing and pounding fear, trying not to forget.

And calm fell again on the city, on the country, as though there had never been a threat. Headlines, after the event, might have been paralysed with fear, but curt voices from the Ministry of Information spoke of control, order, security.

★

Beatrice heaved the water into the field behind the house, rejoiced in the thickness, the goodness of the earth, and the rich smells that came from it. She paused, eyes narrowed against the past, and remembered Benjamin, as a child of two, laughing and eating the yellow earth as Beatrice scolded and watched. Never had she had such pain as when she had borne him. She sighed, cradled her bosom in the cool of the evening, watched the land darken around her, the palms become sharp, black shadows in the growing dusk. A dog barked, and she shivered, turning to go in. No; there were two men beside her, coughing gently and shifting their feet. They were in uniform. They had come silently, unobserved, but Beatrice did not show alarm. She looked for a moment, inclined her head, and indicated with her arm that they should go inside. She knew them.

People in the town had reason to fear these two, Jonathan and Amalek. They knew the laws no one else knew, and could use them against the people if they wanted. Mostly they did not need to; people respected them, gave them what they wanted, pampered them, made them happy, and cursed them secretly for demons, bloodsuckers, spirits of the desert. But Beatrice was a healer, well-known in the district. She knew these men and their families, complacent and arrogant, knew them when they were frightened and whimpering with pain, and so she did not fear them. It was they who shifted nervously with her.

It was her son, Benjamin, Jonathan said. He had been arrested trying to kill the Prime Minister – no, no, no, Amalek broke in, you can't take anything straight, it was the President, the President himself, Mrs Beulah. Your son, Benjamin. Beatrice nodded, her stomach cold, she was sitting now in the chair Abraham had made after they were

84

married. She looked up at the policemen, her eyes shining with puzzlement – and so? what now? You will have to answer questions, Mrs Beulah, the Captain will come tomorrow, and you must go the station. Is your husband here? Beatrice nodded, no. He is away. Always away, like Benjamin. The President? Why should – ? The policemen, Jonathan and Amalek, were embarrassed. Like schoolboys, they wanted to exchange glances and snicker because they could not take the pain in Beatrice's eyes. They knew why Benjamin had tried to kill the President, everybody knew why someone should want to. But Beatrice did not, and did not want to know. Tomorrow, Mrs Beulah, and your husband too, when he comes back. Everybody must be questioned. Beatrice nodded again. The room was dark and still.

On her bed, Beatrice stared without focus and did not hear the coughs, the cries, the barks of the warm night. Towards dawn, when Abraham, her husband, crawled in beside her, she turned to him, and began to whisper into his ear all that was in her heart, feeling him grow cold beside her. At length, she stopped, and turning aside, she slept. Abraham did not sleep, but lay and listened to Beatrice breathing quietly beside him, thinking again all the things he had thought since Benjamin left for the city. Already gone in soul, the young man was listless at home and would not work. He drank beer and spent time flirting with schoolgirls. His eyes were empty and unhappy, and Beatrice, his mother, so skilful at healing others, could do nothing with him. Abraham took him aside and talked to him about life, about his own father, and his father's brothers, how they had fought and travelled and founded families in different parts. He told him how restlessness

and adventure came with youth, and how peace and
tranquillity came with age. But Benjamin laughed and said
father, you have never stopped wandering, you have no
roots of age, you are a tumbleweed, not a tree, how can you
say these things to me your son?

The President sat at his desk and a fly buzzed in the room.
He knew the knife was there. It lay where it had been
dropped two days before. He had not moved it, had not
looked at it, would not allow the office to be cleaned. His
foot itched to kick it out of sight, but he would not. BB.
Benjamin Beulah. A stupid name. A government scholar.
He probably shook my hand once. Is it a plot? Damned
intellectuals!

I admire your spirit, he said to Benjamin, later. He did
not expect a reply. The young man was bloody and puffy
about the face and did not look entirely aware. I do, I
admire it. I had a spirit like yours in my young days. Like
a lion, eh? Still like a lion! Grizzled, but still strong, eh? I
had you going there, didn't I? You thought it would be
easy, an old man, a knife, over in seconds; a dynasty fallen,
a country brought to a halt, fate changed, history in the
balance. One old man dead over a desk. Is that what you
thought? But I work out every day. The papers say so, it's
true. I'm still as strong as a young man. You didn't get me,
I got you. And you're mine. I like you. You're good to talk
to. We will be good friends, you and I, before the end.
Pausing, on his way out of the room, he heaved his fist
deep into the belly of the man bound to the chair. Benjamin
groaned, tried to spit the pain, could not absorb the blow,
the chair was fixed to the floor. He bent forward, passed

out, and the door clicked as the President walked out, flexing his arm.

Take care of him, he's like a son to me, he said to the officer on duty.

When Beatrice found herself alone the next morning, she was not surprised. She had never tamed Abraham, had never really tried to. She accepted his comings and goings, his angers and violence, like a large rock which sees the face of the plain change before it. And yet they were intimate, these two, they knew each other like animals do, they lived and breathed in a single rhythm. Like rock and wind, they coexisted: she, seemingly immutable yet ever changing with the carving of time, he all energy, passage, keen, solitary persistence.

How could two such people have a son? And what would he be? To have him, Abraham and Beatrice had given up the grander delights of their courtship, which had continued long after they were married. Their life together in the early years had been like a dance, he all passion and fire, she solemn warmth, calming, chiding, putting shape to his temperament. The focus, the change, to Benjamin and then to Absalom, had been difficult for Abraham after the initial delight of paternity. Beatrice was not his sole enjoyment, the focus was gone. Abraham had found that early exultation in each other the most difficult to give up.

Absalom. Their first great sorrow, that bound them together like twisted vines. Absalom, their second son, who went out in the bush one day and cut his own throat. Found half eaten by animals, no one knew why. Black, black, day. And trying to keep it from Benjamin, in case he tried to come home, all that way. Absalom, and now Benjamin. Beatrice got up from her bed, stretched, felt the bones creak and the warm blood flow. It seemed as if she lived two lives, one full of horror and sorrow, insurmountable woe, the other, physical, continuous, impregnable. That was what Abraham found so difficult. When Absalom was found, Abraham disappeared into the mountains for five days without food, walking, crying, beating his body into the bones of the earth, sleeping he knew not where, until his delirium had passed. Beatrice stayed at home, washed the body and laid it out, baked the bread for the mourners, and saw Absalom buried in the red earth. And then she sat and wrote the dreadful letter to Benjamin, she who could hardly write. Son. Your brother Absalom. Dead in the bush, his own act. We don't know why. Don't come home. We are well and fine. The rain has not yet come. Mother.

Beatrice, Beatrice, my love, screamed Abraham to the rocks, I love you. Why why why why why why why why why why???? I'll gash myself, I'll wound myself for this loss, but I know that your smooth, plump flesh is more deeply wounded, Beatrice, flesh of your flesh is gone.

Benjamin had come home, in shock, angry at being excluded. He found it all over, silence, fresh red earth already dry and crusted. Home life was intolerable. Beatrice spoke to two zombies, each hating the other. Abraham hating his son for still being alive. Benjamin hating his father as the mysterious cause of his brother's death. The town too remained silent before Benjamin; he frowned in the street, he wore his English clothes and would not stop. After a week, he left again, and people spoke of his distance, how he had changed. As if for a trial, he came home, accusing because he was absent from the scene of the crime, assessing everybody's guilt but his own. He was arrogant, that boy, he would not last long here.

I want his background, Piercy, his friends here in the city, his home town sought out, his family, friends there, questioned. I want to know his guts, I want to know what burns in them, I want to know the colour of his bile, Piercy, am I clear to you, you understand me? His town. Is it local, is it clan rebellion? Is it intellectuals here in the city? Is it CIA, foreign interest? He's been abroad, look out the other scholars, those still here, those abroad. Freeze the funds, frighten them. Tell me a story, Piercy, make me happy when we hang him, let me know it's over, let me know who else to hang. Am I clear? OK, goodbye. The receiver rests. Bloody greasy phone.

Amalek coughed and rolled the tiny ball of newspaper between his toes and the ground. Beatrice watched the ball dully, shifting her fingers. The waiting room was warm. Inside the office, beyond the closed door, there was silence, not the slightest sound. From time to time there was a faint crack, as if someone were shifting position in a chair, but that was all. He's busy, Mrs B., you'll have to wait.

There was a sound from inside the office, a low voice and a laugh. The boards creaked with footsteps and Jonathan opened the door. Mrs Beulah, the Captain will see you. Amalek looked at her idly as she crossed his line of vision, still rolling the ball of paper. Poor cow.

The Captain leans forward, breathes out his smoke in her eyes. She bravely blinks, takes a tighter hold on her fingers. Listen, woman, this is real trouble. This is not crime, this is death. How far will it go, this death? Will it stop at your son, is there treason in your family, in your village? Where will death stop? Madness, insanity we can all understand, we can cope. If it's in the family. Who's to blame if you're harmless, shout at the rocks? Mad dogs, of course, have to be locked up. Eyes narrow. Madness, dear Mrs B., or treason? And how far? I need to know. I will know.

Beatrice shook her grey untidy head. Her voice low. No, Captain, we have no madness in our family, no treason. We keep the laws, your constables will tell you – Jonathan did not respond, he was outside the haze, the magic circle of yellow tobacco smoke – the madness, the treason, is in the world. You can see it, Captain, in the market, when they take your money and look daggers at your back. My son Absalom, I don't know where he found it, it came upon him suddenly when he was alone, and overcame him. Benjamin, I don't know, he went away, and never came back. Someone else came back, called Benjamin. But he too has met the beast in the wilderness, treachery and madness in a foreign place. My husband – don't speak of him, he's not here.

You stupid woman. The slap made her eyes startle, her mouth felt puffy, blood trickled a little from the corner of her lips. The Captain leaned back, was silent, paused for reflection, stubbing out his cigarette. I will see you and your husband again. You will not leave the town. Understood? A query at Jonathan, who nodded, understood boss. Get out.

★

Beatrice rolled her thoughts in her head as she kneaded the dough on the table. Thus and so she would like to knead the flesh of her son, Benjamin. Take her hands to his neck, feel the root of the skull where it swivels on the spine, loosen the knots and spasms that chase his thoughts across the muscles of his head. Dig deep into the shoulders, take out the weariness and pain, read there an unburdening of spirits, a pouring out of what was locked inside. He forbade it. He was a foreigner when he came home. Beatrice could see the haemorrhage in his heart, could feel it in herself. There was no medium between them. Nothing passed by way of communication between them. He would not look at her.

One day, before he left, she reached out as he passed her in the slanted light from the window and grasped his arm. He stood, and waited for her to let go. And so she did. They were mute. They had found the uttermost limits of love and closure. There was nothing they could do for the other, nothing that they could share. And yet, they suffered equally from it. They were bound together all the more strongly by their helplessness in the face of it.

In this morning light, as Beatrice made bread alone in the house, she wept. A child eating dust looked up and laughed. The tears fell as if to fill the chasm in her heart. A child, charming forever and eternally lost.

Beatrice stood panting at the doorpost of her back door, bent forward, one hand on her knee, the other pushed firmly against the post. Behind her, the bloated body of the poisoned goat stank horribly. She had tried to pull it through the dust to the end of the field and burn it, but her strength had given out. This is what it is to be suddenly old. Behind her, the field stretched like foreign territory. Out there, she was in the open, exposed to the hostile absence of her neighbours. Tugging at the legs of the goat, she had sat down, gasping, but there was neither mirth nor comment from the watchers, invisible in their houses.

Inside the house, Abraham moaned with fever. On the morning of that day, she had sat by his side and wiped his brow with a white cloth. In a moment, even as her hand caressed his forehead, she felt a chill passing through her hands and arms. Without knowing how it was, she knew the feeling, she sat back and stared blankly at her hands. Her healing power was gone. She felt no longer confident in her ministrations, but frightened, terrified by the spectre of illness before her. It sat in Abraham's body, no longer afraid of her and submissive to her commands, but sly, vicious, ready to bite anyone who came near. It was as if all the sickness she had ever cast out was stored up in the sweating body of Abraham, waiting for a final victory.

In the night, Abraham in his delirium heard the voices that prowled round the house, whispering and tapping, laughing at their courage.

Abraham crouched in the field, shivering, and staring at the flames that devoured the house. Between him and the house was the sharp silhouette of a man with a stick. He wore no uniform, but it looked like Amalek. On the fringes of the light there were other men, all looking inward towards the light. Abraham didn't know how he had got there. He had been dreaming of walking in the wilderness, in the mountains to the north, but this was no dream.

Beatrice was not near. Oh, Beatrice. In the red depths framed by door and windows, there was nothing distinct to be seen. Were there human sounds from inside the house, a high-pitched shriek in the midst of cracking wood and smashing glass? Was that Beatrice's figure standing in the midst of the flames, her head a halo of light? The flames licked on, there was no sound or movement to satisfy the watchers. Someone threw another bottle filled with kerosene, a woman laughed. Soon, it would be over, and they would return to their homes. In the morning they would sift through the ashes and look for bones. Meanwhile, the fascination of fire held them captive. Abraham bent his head to the soil, and wept. He saw Beatrice as he had left her, lying on their bed, the lines on her face erased by sleep. Beatrice.

When dawn came, Abraham was on the highway, walking, head up. He was going to the city to see what they had done with his son.

When Abraham first dreamt that his mythical ancestor was talking to him, he was lying in the bush by the Barifa highway. It was the third night of his journey; he lay with his head on a stone, and above him the stars glittered, impossibly bright. The cicadas chirped in crowded rhythm; there was no outward sign to mark the moment.

It was on just such a night as this, he said, that I began my journey, called out from my home by I know not what blind craving, and into just such a wilderness as this. This said carefully looking round, and taking in the moony landscape with ancient eyes, surveying it, considering and weighing each part of it, as the visible part only of a vast land of mountain ranges and rivers, bitter lakes, dry savannah, forest and crusty field, extending in every direction to more land and then to the sea.

We did not have drought; no war, no famine, no hunger, no plague or sorrow to haunt us. We had no spiritual ill. We had all that might be expected or hoped for, and yet we came out, we came out to this wilderness to fall victim to its deceits. The old man paused, as if for breath. And I remember, the stars shone just as brightly on that first night as they do tonight. There may have been a tear in the old man's eye, Abraham could not tell. But there was a jewel-like intensity to the silence that remained when the old man had gone.

All night long, Abraham thought of what his ancestor had said. As dawn grew he began to get cold, and got up, stamping hard and clasping himself tight. He gathered some sticks and sat down to a small fire. The sun entered the world swiftly; his fire grew pale and insignificant, and he let it burn out. The morning smelled pungent. Abraham unwrapped a piece of the bread he had begged on the way, and began to chew, facing the sky where the day grew stronger. The birds began to fly.

Later, Abraham gathered together his bundle and his staff, and rejoined the highway. He was a wild figure now, as self-contained as a wound-up spring, with features deeply graved, a shock of grey hair and distressing eyes. He would remain self-contained when, later in the morning, the grinding lorry crowded with sixty laughing soldiers thundered past in the choking dust, the driver leaning crazily out of the battered door to curse and chaff him.

Shortly before noon his ancestor spoke to him again. This is like the land in which I buried my wife, he said. The boulders were piled in such and such a way, as if tumbled together in a game of the gods or some mighty earthquake, though in reality they floated there in a great flood. Abraham saw that he was pointing to the craggy escarpment to the east of the road. Out of it gazed an ancient skull, a trick of the sunlight cast across caverns. A bird clattered out of a tree behind them, and circling once, flew away to the distant hills.

I bought the land to bury her in from the elders of a village nearby. It was not easy to persuade them, for they did not think the spirits of the place would take kindly to a foreigner among them. I gave them gold and told them I would put my wife in a cave and seal her up. They watched me, made sure that I did, and then they made me leave, telling me not to return.

He walked on for a while with Abraham, who was thinking, Beatrice, Beatrice. He did not notice when his companion left him again.

When, in late afternoon, Abraham walked into Tabra town, there was tattered bunting fluttering in the hot wind which came off the plain. It was hung across the road at intervals from the place where the dirt road ended and the pitted macadam began, and it continued with weary festivity as far into the town as the eye cared to chase it. It was strung from trees where huge pelicans squatted and brayed and sometimes raised their wings and hunched their heads. There were few people about at the outskirts of town; some fruitsellers by the roadside, idlers, schoolboys, women carrying water. Abraham sat in the shade of a tree and accepted the orange he was offered. Before him life proceeded peacefully and anonymously. He rested.

When we first began to wander, his ancestor said, we were young, and my wife was beautiful. In every place we went, the chief men of the place wanted to take her from me, for the colour of her skin was different, and they had exotic tastes. They caused me much trouble, these men, and in the end I told my wife to cover her face and avert her eyes, and thereafter it seemed to me that the sun ceased to shine upon the earth. Silence fell again, and Abraham spat in the dust.

The fruitseller who had given him the orange looked at him with a quizzical eye. You have been travelling for a long time, he said. Abraham did not look or respond. The police here, they are looking for an old man on foot or hitching lifts in lorries. They say he is dangerous. Abraham looked at the man who spoke. A poor man, friendly enough, it seemed. It might be risky for such a man to go farther into town, the fruitseller continued, all strangers are being questioned. They say such a man might well hide in the rocks just north of town. Who would know that he was there? As he spoke, the man was wrapping up his wares into a large bundle, for it was getting late. He left two large yams and a straw mat on the site, and stood up. He hesitated for a moment, looking down at Abraham, who stared back, not uttering a word. Go well, father, the fruitseller said, and humping his sack as he turned, he began to walk away up the road. Abraham watched him go. He felt very tired.

Towards nightfall, Abraham followed the man's advice and walked out to the tumbled rocks that lay above the

town, carrying the mat and the fruit. He began to climb,
seeking a high place to rest, and sleep. He had left it late;
night was shutting in, he stumbled on the rocks and was
afraid of scorpions. Here at night all things became black,
he thought.

Abraham's breathing came hard. At length he settled on
a level spot between two large rocks, and he laid out the
mat and tried to rest. Around him he could hear the whir
of insects and from the huts that marked the edge of town
and the edge of wilderness, there came the quick noise of
children squabbling on their clay beds, and the long, low
sound of men talking and laughing together. Dogs with
large submissive eyes paced the red dust again and again,
nosing for scraps, waiting for darkness and a certain
measure of pride.

I lied, came the quiet voice of his ancestor, when I said
there was no spiritual ill to drive us out of our country. It
was a beautiful country, fertile beyond imagining. All that
was planted flourished, and the people and the cattle were
sleek and fat. We loved the land, we ploughed our strength
and virility into it; we tended and decorated it; we built
great palaces and gardens, jewels set in a rich landscape.
But the land did not love us. The fat of the land stuck in
our craw. There was a hardness, an unfriendly brightness
in the manicure of the gardens of the princes. The land sat
waiting, waiting until we were gone. How could we admit
that the evil, the dissatisfaction lay in our own hearts? How
could we accept this unease with which the land of our
dreams filled us? A land that was so inviting, so satisfying
in material goods, so liberal with its beauty and fragrance,
and yet which seemed to withhold from us its final assent,
like a mistress that turns down the corners of her mouth

involuntarily at the appearance of the suitor she does not love.

When we saw this, we had to leave, and quickly, in the night. And all through our wanderings, we have not been able to understand why we should have been treated so, why God should have done this thing to us.

When the drone of his ancestor's voice had ceased, Abraham turned and slept. As the moon rose high and the dogs snarled in the town below, Abraham began to dream. It was daytime, and he was standing as a young man on a great height with his father beside him. Beneath them lay stretched out the whole country as Abraham had never seen it before, a land of green made golden by the sun, of cool waters reviving the thirsty earth, of skilled irrigation and tree-shaded canals, of graceful minarets and sun-warmed houses shining white in the landscape. But his father was gone, without a word or a blessing. How to look after this treasure, how to care for it alone? Below him, in the rocks, Abraham saw with shock that his son Absalom squatted, weeping, clasping his throat and rocking to and fro. Before his eyes, the plain was drying and burning. From this distance, there came the faint bellowing of cattle as they tossed thistles with their horns, swinging their heads hopelessly for a glimpse of grass and hope of life. Below him, Absalom was crying, what have they done to me, what have they done to me? The guilt and pain were too much; Abraham roared with the force of it, and striking his head on a stone, awoke. He saw the moon, and the stars, and he breathed deeply the cool air of the night. It was time to cease his internal weeping, it was time to banish mourning. Only Barifa lay before him now.

★

It's a dark night over Barifa. The sky is wide across the plain, torn clouds advance from horizon to horizon. The winds are fitful and gusty.

It was still only an hour after dawn when Abraham bounced into the outer suburbs of Barifa on the back of a Ford flatback truck. The journey across the plain in the early morning had been a great mystery for him; the towers of Barifa glittering in the light that streamed horizontally across the wild grassland reminded Abraham of his dream, and for a while he forgot the purpose of his journey and stared, rapt at the vision, clinging for dear life to the sides of the truck.

Dream ended and reality began again for Abraham when the truck stopped in a dusty street of Makemola suburbs. Barifa, magical Barifa was still some kilometres distant.

It was while resting by the road in Marbeya that Abraham read a tattered sheet of newspaper lying in the long, dry grass of the verge. A hand of death came down on him; battered traffic roared around him, but he sat in ignorance of it, his eyes trying to make sense of the small, printed paragraph: A suspected terrorist, Benjamin J. J. Beulah, was found hanged in his cell yesterday. Beulah, 22, of no fixed abode, was arrested three weeks ago for his involvement in a plot against the President. A police spokesman said that Beulah had shown signs of depression. They are treating the case as suicide.

Abraham let the paper fall, and bent his head to the earth beneath him. In the movements of the ants among the long stems he sought another answer, and found it. In

99

the earth beneath the oil and litter, he saw the earth of his ancestors, the plain by the great river where they had wandered on raids and herded their cattle. He felt the presence of men standing behind him, at his shoulders, carrying their spears and joking at the distance to be run. Old man, we go raiding; one of our people is killed, and they spit in our faces and say he was his own enemy. Father, will you bless us? Will you come?

Abraham snorted, his face flushed with blood as he stabbed the earth with his staff and levered himself to his feet. The people mistook the look in his eyes for madness, and let him pass.

It was time now for the President to go to the grandstand. All white and stiff and fitted out with medals, he stepped with his entourage into the private courtyard of the palace. The heat of the sun hit him hard; he blinked. Across the courtyard a figure was running towards him, white hair flying wild, but running like an athlete.

The President stepped back and looked around. It seemed he was alone, no one within reach. He wasn't ready. He struggled with his sword, pulled it out, held the tip before him, warding. The old man did not notice it. He continued running, his flesh melting through the blade, until, resting with a gasp against the President's chest, he panted and pushed in the bright steel knife, through the white uniform and under the medals, as far as the President's heart.

The two old men looked at each other. The President turned painfully, still supporting Abraham, and with a sigh accepted the end. The two of them fell to the ground, blood staining the sand.

The officers stood around and wondered what they might do next.

And God Gives
Nuts To Those Who
Have No Teeth

John Townsend

It's true!

It is!

That God gives nuts to those who have no teeth!

It must be true. The man told me so himself. Well, all right, not me directly, but he might just as well have done, because he told a friend of mine, a very good friend, a friend who can be implicitly trusted, a friend who wouldn't lie to me, just like I wouldn't lie to you, because I'm your friend. Really I am. A friend being someone who wouldn't lie to you. So you can believe me. Because we're pals, bosom buddies, all that. You say we've never met? Well, you'll just have to take my word for it then, won't you. Like I take my friend Vincent's word. And you wouldn't want to call any friend of mine a liar. No sirree. At least, not if your tiny head is screwed on correctly. Otherwise I might be round your house with my blunt objects. My sharp objects. My objects that are neither blunt nor sharp but will still represent a serious attack on your good health and peace of mind. So just believe me, all right? And things will be hunky-dory. Sure as I'm riding this bike. This is a true story.

Now Vincent was down on his luck. He didn't have a brass farthing, though even if he had, I don't see what use a brass farthing could have been to him. Skint, insolvent, stony broke. He had a ramshackle flat in Queer Street and even there the rent was overdue.

Hot on the heels of poverty breathed hunger. He hadn't had a square meal in days. He wanted one. It didn't even have to be square. Any shape would be acceptable. Triangular. Trapezoid. Rhomboidal even. His stomach kept sending up requests but nothing came back down his throat by way of reply and his innards were beginning to think he'd gone deaf.

For the fourteenth time that day he scoured the kitchen for anything, knowing that there was nothing but still hoping that some morsel might have been overlooked. Perhaps the mice might have taken pity on him and brought something back.

Hunger can make you do some funny things all right. Vincent, he eulogised the fridge. Oh fridge, he sang, how fine you were, in your heyday, in your piping time, overstuffed with Tesco's finest, fine and superfine, the sides of beef, the boxes of wine, the days when I had to squash things to force them into your icebox, when I had to take things out of you to find what I was looking for. But now the golden age is gone, the woods of Arcady are dead. How could I have eaten everything out of you? How could I have sucked you dry? Now all that remains is a part of the wrapper from a packet of frozen peas and a carton of rancid milk which I don't like to throw away because then you would be truly empty, finally, completely void. Standing here like Old Mother Hubbard, but dogless, a strange sadness overtakes me. Pardon me while I shed a few tears on your greasy secondhand door.

When he had finished crying over the fridge Vincent moved on to the cupboards. Now you can't really eulogise cupboards the way you can refrigerators, but you can still try and engage them in conversation. He opened them all up to reveal a few items only of the kind that are inedible by themselves. What is mustard without ham, he asked rhetorically, vinegar without chips, sage without onions. He asked the cupboards these questions, and they replied, nothin;, which he took to be a sign of their complicity. They wouldn't have said anything anyway, but you get the idea, you see the direction in which Vincent was heading.

Ignoring the cries of distress from his stomach he went back into the living room and sat down on the floor, on the threadbare carpet. Why did people spend money on carpets? You couldn't eat carpets. You couldn't make anything out of them. Perhaps he could roll it up and sell it, like he already had all the smaller items. Except he'd never get it past the landlord, who lived on the ground floor, and was always in, ear to the wall. And frankly it was rubbish anyway, so who'd buy it? The man in the moon was who, and Vincent didn't know how to get in touch with him.

So you say, I thought you said Vincent was a friend of yours? And I say, dead right, I did. So you say, why didn't he come to you then, and say, friend, feed me. Because I'm a tight bastard and well known and proud of it, that's why. And also, handouts never help anybody. Suffering is character-building. Good for the soul, which may well be all you're left with, of course, after you starve to death. If souls exist, and there's one way to find out. Okay? All right, then, you say, why didn't Vincent steal? In the face of such desperation? Surely not fear of getting caught, not at this stage, he'd probably only get a fine, if he's a first offender. I should tell you that Vincent has already served three months for grand-theft Meccano. All right then, prison even, what's to fear, when prison gets you three meals a day? And I say, he wasn't completely daft, of course he'd thought of stealing, he wasn't new to that game, even walked into a shop in his biggest overcoat, also his only, hoping to conceal sundry edible items in the sleeves. But the shopkeeper gave him a certain look, and he remembered the ten commandments, and knew they were stupid, in the circumstances, but still they commanded him, all the same, or at least one did, number eight to be precise, a terrible thing, it had never happened to him before, he shuffled out of the shop empty-handed. Poor old Vincent, no conquering for him, despite his handle. Perhaps then you think we should find him out on the city streets, searching the litter bins with the other guys, but Vincent also has a morbid fear of dirt and germs, and couldn't even give it a try. The Social Services? He has already spent what they gave him, on Meccano, of which he is a compulsive buyer, and he isn't due another Giro for almost two weeks. And like I say, I am his friend, and also his only friend, and I am mean. I reckon, if you have to spend all your state handouts on Meccano, well then, don't come crying to me for want of a pork chop. And then you say something else disagreeable, and I say, shut up, who's telling this story anyway.

So Vincent sat on the threadbare carpet surrounded by fantastic Meccano shapes – the guy's an artist, all right? – dreaming of baked beans on toast. Why did he buy

Meccano? Meccano was as bad as the carpet, you couldn't eat that either. But the artist must have his medium. Did Picasso scrimp on canvas because he needed a croque monsieur? Did Henry Miller forego paper for a ham sandwich? Very probably. But then, they weren't stupid.

Most of Vincent's recent constructions were representations of food, as thoughts of food were all that filled his head, and his head was where the constructions came from. His mashed potatoes with sausages sticking out, you know, like they do it in the *Beano* and your mum would never let you, Jimmy, don't play with your food, smack, was particularly elegant. He'd make something else, but he'd used up all the bits already, and he never liked to deconstruct in case he forgot how he'd done it in the first place. But time has to be passed so he switched on the television, sadly already knowing what was coming up.

Snap crackle and pop! Bootiful! The Oxo family! A tip: if you're ever hungry and without the wherewithal to purchase food, don't watch the adverts. He tried the non-commercial stations. On one, *The Food Programme*. On the other, *Farmers' Weekly*. He imagined various innocent domestic animals roasting, frying, crackling, a vegetarian's nightmare, but not for Vincent, if a pig had strolled past at that moment, he'd have snapped a chunk out of it, no problem.

He turned off the TV. Sell the TV! You fool! But it was rented. And anyway, you have to have one. Otherwise you might miss Bob Monkhouse's latest witticism, or being horrified by the disgraceful left-wing bias of the news coverage, always the same, reds in talking heads' clothing, bastards, every station. I mean, there are some things you just can't afford to be without in this world, and television would appear to be one of them.

Oh God thought Vincent staring blankly at a very realistic Meccano sculpture of cheese on toast. God? God? Worth a try. Pray to the old bastard. Now, despite his parentally hammered-in occasionally surfacing allegiance to the ten commandments, Vincent was no creeping Jesus. Far from it. He went with girls to whom he wasn't married, stole Meccano – just the once – and shopped on Sundays. But in the circumstances, you know, prayer, it was usually circumstances that made anybody do it, whatever they might say. Dear God, he began. But no crawling, please.

Dear God, he said out loud, getting onto his knees, getting his hands into the customary position. The missionary position? No such luck. Dear God, he said again, you know I don't ask for much. Much? Much? He caught himself just as he started falling. What is this meek and mild crap! Too right I don't ask for much. I ASK FOR EVERYTHING! But just for now, something to eat will do, *now* he shouted. If that's not too much effort for you, if you can take a break from judging sinners or suffering little children or whatever it is you get up to are you listening? Vincent got up off his knees and circled the room, carefully avoiding his constructions and getting louder by the minute. Come on, come on, I'm ready for you, I'm hot, I'm hungry, let's see what you can do. Is there anybody out there? Room service! Send me some food! I don't care what it is except please nothing to do with celery and make it clean can you? Fried chicken would be nice. Or paella, any kind of seafood. I'm really into fish. Do you take orders? I'll have a number twenty-three! And no tricks, you'd better call in person, or at least send an angel. I want to see if you deliver. Manna from heaven toute-suite! Save me, and I mean my stomach not my soul. You're the man with the mercy. Whip it out. Get it on. Bang the dinner gong. Come on God! Biscuits gravy rice pudding garlic bread pizza macaroni cheese. You're my last chance, you wouldn't catch me praying otherwise! Ham eggs spam vegetables. GREAT STEAMING GOBBETS OF RAW DRIPPING BRUISY FLESH! BUCKETS OF GREAT SCALY LIVE AND GASPING SLITHERING FLOPPING FISH! EELS! EELS! MEALS ON WHEELS! FEED ME! GET ME OUT OF THIS!

Vincent raved on shouting great lists of hyperbolic food at the ceiling and might have still been doing so to this day and from here on into eternity had he not been interrupted by the ringing of the doorbell. He quickly put on some clothes and hurried down the stairs to answer it.

There was a little old man standing on the step holding an empty wine bottle in one hand and a brown paper bag of something in the other. You called? he said.

Vincent thought, you're the one ringing the doorbell.

No, you did.

No, you called me.

What?

I'm God, can I come in?

Vincent grabbed him and pulled him over the threshold. He didn't want the neighbours seeing God standing on his doorstep. The embarrassment! And him an atheist. That was if the neighbours recognised God of course. Which probably none of them would. Not even if he walked up and bit them. Which he probably wouldn't. What with them mostly being practising theists of one sort or another and, so far as Vincent could tell, none of them very good at it. That old chestnut. And also assuming the man was who he said he was, which would be a big assumption, but Vincent could be pretty big when it came to assuming things, at least in the first instance. It was the fifteenth of August, an obscure religious joke. Later on he could be difficult.

Upstairs said Vincent. I know said the man and went up with Vincent following him and straight into the right flat without even a pause for directions or consideration. Sit down, said Vincent, fully aware that there wasn't so much as a chair or a stool or a pouffe in the room or anything else comparable in function.

On what?

The floor. What else is there?

At my age? And me with rheumatism and arthritis and who knows what else? No thanks. The old man made artistic motions with his hands and then sat down on the resulting sofa.

How did you do that? said Vincent.

I said, I'm God. It's the sort of thing I do. A man needs a calling. I've come to answer your prayers.

How do I know you're God?

You can materialise furniture?

You could be the other feller.

Trust me.

Why not, thought Vincent, and, what can I lose, and, why spurn a possible source of amusement.

Why did you come?

I told you, to answer your prayers.

You call that praying?

Near enough.

And you come to everyone who prays?

Certainly not. I like your style. God materialised a cigarette in his mouth and lit it with a fingertip. I hate your meek and mild types, just ignore them as a rule. I'm like your British Civil Service, you want to get anything done, you have to make a lot of noise. Dig the sculptures by the way. Any luck?

Not really.

Too far-out I suppose. Here. God held out his brown paper bag. These are for you.

Vincent took the bag and looked inside. Nuts. A bag of nuts. Walnuts, brazil nuts, hazel nuts, almonds. Shit. Just like Christmas. Nuts. He should have said, along with celery. In fact, now that he thought about it, when it came to him and food, there were a lot of things that were no good. His face fell. God caught it.

What's up? No crackers?

Worse. No teeth.

Surely you've got some false ones?

I accidentally dropped them into the last begging letter I wrote to my mum and posted it before I realised. Now she won't return them, says they're better than her own.

Oh. Sorry.

Haven't you got anything else?

They were all I could find. See, we don't usually eat up there, not real stuff, somebody slipped these into my Christmas stocking for an amusing touch of authenticity. I've been hanging on to them ever since.

So couldn't you just whistle something up?

Nothing substantial. This sofa, me, my cigarette, they're all just illusions. I don't think illusory food is what you're after. Not very filling.

Nothing at all? Vincent's face was now parallel with the floor.

Really, not a sausage. Oh except, God rummaged around in the pocket of his shabby overcoat. Just this. He held out a wilting stick of celery.

You useless old sod!

Vincent got up off the floor and took a trial swing at God but his fist went straight through him and he fell over into a sculpture of strawberry cheesecake.

Well thanks, he said, thanks a lot. The next time I think of praying, remind me to stick my head in a bucket instead. God smiled beatifically as only God could. Vincent took his supposedly working model reconstruction of an M16, a beautiful piece, done in his Vietnam period, aimed it at God and squeezed the trigger. Well what do you know, it fired. The bullet flew straight through God and the sofa and ricocheted off Vincent's *Blue Cheese on a Half-Shell*, his brilliant Meccano reference to Botticelli's Venus, and from there shot out the window where it scored a direct hit right between the eyes of a Conservative MP who just happened to be crossing the road outside during the action.

Oh well, said Vincent, at least I can return the gift. You'll have something useless to take back with you now.

I think I should have kept the nuts, said God.

The spirit of the deceased flew into the room. God squeezed it into the empty wine bottle, stuck a cork in, put it in his pocket.

Still, he'll probably go to the other place.

A small crowd was gathering in the street. Sirens wailed. The police arrived.

Why? said Vincent,. Why why why? Why did you have to give me nuts?

Well, you know what they say.

What?

God smiled and did the Cheshire cat bit, fading away till he was just a grin. Water is a boon in the desert, he said, but the drowning man curses it. And God gives nuts to those who have no teeth. Then even the grin was gone.

Vincent threw a last punch but there was nothing left to hit, not that it would have done him any good anyway, like thumping air.

And then he came to see me.

I have by the way a confession to make. That bit was lies. That bit about the Meccano M16 and shooting the MP and God putting his soul in a bottle, though I have it on good authority that that is the kind of thing he does, I made it up. Just testing you. Didn't it strike you, as you were reading it, as being just a little unlikely? But it proves the rest is true. Otherwise, if I was lying, why admit to making a part of it up? The rest is just as Vincent told it, more or less, literary embellishments aside, but they're allowable, licence, poetic or otherwise. OK? God's truth, and like I say, he wouldn't lie to me, and I wouldn't lie to you, not without telling you, so there it is.

Vincent came to me and said, Got anything to eat?

And I said, Who's paying?

He offered me one of his sculptures. No thanks, I said. Too far-out. I've got a good story, he said. A beautiful story, and true. The two go together, as you'll probably have heard. Let's hear it, I said, being a sucker for a good yarn, especially if it's on the level. He told it. I was impressed. He let me have it for a tin of creamed rice pudding and some black bananas. Remember, no teeth.

And now I'm passing it on to you. But nothing is free. Mine's a tuna fish salad sandwich made with wholemeal bread, and please go easy on the mayonnaise.

Re-Possessed

Rosemary Mackay

'I'll just leave you, then . . . ?'

From the passenger-seat, George glanced at his son's face, the mixture of concern, sadness and eagerness to be released there, causing the stilled grief to push upwards against his chest: 'I've been here often enough before, haven't I?' he replied, with a gruffness he hadn't intended. He wanted to be released as well, but every change of scene these past days was a temporary expedient, more draining of his reserves than he had imagined possible. He had to get through it, they all had; but it was his future days which were uncertain, his road which had forked.

George fumbled for the catch to his seat-belt, anticipating a similar, redundant action by his son. A quick flash of anger made him gasp with exasperation. They both heard it as a sigh.

'You're sure . . . ?'

Again, George imagined Jim unfastening himself and he snapped: 'Sure. I'm fine.'

The car door was open and George heaved himself onto

the familiar pavement, slammed the door behind him and almost stopped in his tracks. The house was different. What was it? He forced his feet forward, running his eyes across its façade, through the small patch of front garden, back up to the roof. Jim's car revved up, shifted gear and became any car as it turned the corner. George did not want to enter his own front door until he had identified the alteration; but the dread of observing new behaviour in himself urged him on.

Inside the narrow, dark hallway, the air was musty in a way it had never been and he moved his large body through the silence, tentatively, feeling the muscles in his calves cramp: he was tip-toeing.

'For God's sake,' he said aloud, placing his feet flat on the carpet as he pushed open the living-room door.

'It's my house,' he thought. '*My* house.' But his eyes darted across the floor into the corners, penetrating shadows, chasing the sound he had made.

His breath hung in the air before him, but his face was warm, his palms sweaty, his breathing rapid. Normality: he had to impose routine, do the things here he always did. Suddenly, he understood why everyone stolidly concentrated on the small things at these times: it kept the fear away. Necessary arrangements filled entire days, from the ordering of the coffin, down to the detail of which hymns to sing; from the burial of the body to the question of what to put in the sandwiches. And a constant stream of people, anyone who ever knew her, starting in childhood and ending with the assistant in the baker's shop at the precinct. Each one had assumed an importance; taking his hand, the tears sparkling in their eyes as they held his gaze, in a way which he had begun to resent. They thought that grief was to share, like that large cake Jim's wife had insisted was essential, when George wanted only the individual sand-wiches; each to his own.

This last ritual was his, to be performed alone, the decision about what to keep. He was going to live with Jim and Mary, married for years, with a house full of belong-ings. Mary had suggested that his 'own' room could be furnished with movables from home, but as he fastened on single pieces, they seemed tawdry in the context of Jim's modern, fashionable place.

He removed his overcoat and sat down on the nearest chair, ignoring the one at the fireside which he had used routinely for years. One hand automatically explored his side pocket for his pipe, until he remembered. In an effort to cut down, he had left his pouch behind. A smoke would have helped. Less than a week since he had switched off the electricity and carried his suitcases out to Jim's waiting car. In that time, the house had eased him out, had drawn the wraps around itself and turned its face away. It wasn't his house, never had been, despite the name on the ownership deed. He had returned here expecting to have to extricate himself from the house's claim upon him and the house had already set him free, pre-empted his choice.

Betty had owned the house. He had never known anyone who could own like she could: she possessed things, took them to herself, knew them in an intimate and excluding way. The everyday basis had been pointed enough. He could return from work one evening to find that some undeniable possession had taken place: a settee re-covered and the proof, in the shape of an ashtray full of pennies, pens, buttons and badges, that she had been up to her armpits in it. In his imagination, he would see her huge bulk balanced on the seat, one hand gripping the back of the settee while the other groped in the guts of the thing, her face flushed with the excitement of the hunt.

The annual spring-clean could bring him to the verge of an anxiety state, as she stripped down windows, disembow-elled cupboards, turned mattresses, beat rugs. Even the lamps could not escape: their heads would come off, their trunks standing exposed for the pummelling they were to undergo, sometimes their flexes explored for bare parts, her large hand pawing the stem with sensitised fingertips.

He had tried, when he was a child, to have secret, special things of his own. In the small, overcrowded flat he shared with his family, he read of space in books, of boys his age who cherished belongings and he yearned to know the feeling. Once or twice he practised, with his yo-yo or a favourite knife, concealing it in the corner of a drawer, staring at it for minutes, trying to give it that significance he had read of, before someone burst into the room, and he hastily closed the drawer. Next day, remembering suddenly, half-way through the morning, he would return to the drawer to find nothing more than the thing itself, a tin yo-yo with knots in the string and a dent caused when a bigger boy in the playground had seized it and thrown it against a stone. It was beyond him, this possessing business.

He went into the kitchen. It was partly that, of course: with the electricity shut off, the kitchen appliances didn't make their live sounds. No clicking on of the fridge, no vibration of a small motor, no quiet roar of a kettle coming to the boil. His eyes skimmed the mantelshelf: the latest postcard from their daughter, Stella, in Vancouver, already gone back there; the battery which he had removed from

Re-Possessed

the smoke-detector because its piercing bleep upset Betty in her last weeks; a packet of Disprin kept handy for the headaches which plagued his nights; incongruous ornaments which Betty had dusted, polished, re-arranged and claimed.

It was junk, all of it, things without significance, lacking the beauty in Betty's gaze. He had wanted rid of it all, had suggested that the rubbish-tip was the best place for it: 'What's the use in keeping cheap, utility furniture? We only bought it for want of something better at the time,' he would argue, aware of his ulterior motive for a new beginning.

Betty had frustrated him. Unable to out-argue him, she had simply dug her heels in, redoubled her home-making output, sewn him up in a new floral-pattern cover for his easy-chair. He stared at it now, willing back the anger he had felt at the time. But Betty had manoeuvred herself out of that one as well. He knew that when the grief and confusion of loss went, a rearranged Betty would take shape in his mind, re-covered and virtually unrecognisable. Not new, just different and, like the house, no longer his own. Instead of the old hurt, his mind would assume Betty's version of herself, the face which she presented to the world and which hid the threadbare, the tatty, the worn-out. Betty would take possession of herself.

Above the fireplace was a tapestry, one of hers done at a night class. She had hinted that he join up, attend a class in joinery or home decorating, but too late once the kids were up and away. Mary was just as bad. He saw all the signs, the look of rapt concentration when her eyes slewed round her living-room. Probably, it was some disorder that all women suffered from; an extension of the nesting instinct distorted by human development. He didn't want to go through it all again with another woman.

Restless to be free of his thoughts, he pushed himself out of the armchair and stood up. Where could he go? He turned his head in the direction of the hallway, then quickly away. He should be shoving all Betty's clothes into refuse bags, saving Mary a lot of extra work, but already he had the smell of her in his nostrils and he was afraid that the touch might be too much.

'I could forgive her,' he thought. 'Forgive her for dying.'

His mouth twisted in a grimace: 'Bloody nonsense,' he told himself. 'The poor woman didn't want to die.' That, if nothing else, had been plain to see.

There had been recriminations, anger at him for being the one healthy enough to do the nursing: 'Who would have thought you'd be the one to survive, with all the drinking and smoking you've done?' she had said, trying to smile, with her mouth shaping into that ghastly pout which the steroids had caused, the hatred in her eyes making something inside him wither with misery, the denial of desire for his own life lodged in the middle of his chest. You didn't deny life at times like that; no one beckoned death when it was there, with you, in the back of a cupboard or lurking in the shadows, in case it pounced and caught the wrong person.

Now, he felt that enough dying had been done. He had been led to respect death, as a momentous thing, a breath away, in the same sense that others believed God to be, ubiquitous, omniscient, fearful.

He was in the hallway, staring at the turn on the stairs: maybe if he started on the bathroom, with its synthetic odours, he could then graduate to the bedroom smells. He decided that he needed the toilet anyway, so he armed himself with the roll of black bags he'd carried with him in his overcoat pocket and headed for the stairs.

In front of the bathroom cabinet he stood dropping bottles and tins into a bag, telling himself that there was nothing to it, surprised at the speed his hands were moving. He had decided to sell the house with everything left intact, more or less, but he could see already as he moved things, that rings stained the painted shelves. It would have to be cleaned. He shifted his attention to the bath, refusing to be affected by the intimate items such as sponges, face-cloths, his breath loud in his ears as he bent and stretched. It was right that the house should die with Betty, that he should make way for a new set of people to revive it.

A dull thud from the bedroom next door made his hand freeze in mid-air, inches from the shampoo.

'She's there. She's come back.'

He stared at the tiles on the wall round the bath, not breathing, waiting, he realised, for her shout. He didn't want to hear it. He didn't want her back, not ill, not prolonging those dreadful last days. Then, he thought: 'Maybe she's come back from the grave.'

His outstretched hand began to shake, his heart thumping against his ribs, choking him. In terror, he took a huge gulp of air and the geometric pattern on the tiles danced and flickered.

'Get a bloody grip, man,' he told himself, letting the bag drop with a crash onto the linoleum, and strode into the hall.

He threw open the bedroom door: nothing. All as he had left it, except for the mustiness which was everywhere. He had never thought of the house as being damp and felt a bright relief at the realisation that the responsibility was no longer his to deal with. He glanced over at the closed wardrobe, the chest of drawers. There was no need for him to go into the business. His sister, Molly, would want to stake a claim, would be delighted at the opportunity to wade unsupervised through all the paraphernalia.

'Then let her. Let them all,' he thought. He wasn't interested in being part of these people's lives any more, was tired of the kind of interference they thought of as fond interest in him. He wanted to be left alone, not drawn around their hearths, given a place at their table, a bed in their room.

'Dammit, I won't go!' he said aloud and his mind filled with possibilities. There was an Old Folk's Home three streets away, segregated, except for eating and TV-watching, where he'd visited his old friend, Johnny Robertson, a widower himself. In an institution like that, everything was owned by the Council. All you had was a few token, personal effects.

Excitement stirred thoughts of what to take, but a calmness slowed his breathing, cooled his cheeks and dried his palms. Books were what he had always loved, having a life of their own which challenged you to take them or leave them. He studied the books on the bookcase behind the bedroom door. Quickly, with a confidence which surprised him, he made his selection: *The Complete Works of Shakespeare* in a single volume, never read but held over to a later date, various works by Sir Walter Scott, and the most recent photograph album of his grandchildren. He resisted the idea of his Gladstone bag and dropped the books into one of his black bags. There was just the announcement to Jim and he was at liberty to go, travelling light.

Downstairs, at the living-room door, he turned a last smile on the room, then felt a guilty tremor when he spotted Betty smiling happily back at him: the photograph of their Golden Wedding celebration. He'd better take it: it wouldn't do for his pals to think him a bachelor, not with all his grandchildren trooping in to visit. His pals, with not a scrap to call their own, but a few pieces of clothing and the old biddies knitting up belongings as fast as they could. He visualised the Council-owned sitting-room, the Council-owned carpet, curtains, chairs, TV, pictures, magazines, and he chuckled to himself at the thought of the place waiting for him and his pension.

On the pavement, George turned and looked at the house for the last time. It *was* different, quite different, not singular or distinctive in the merest detail. There were rows of them, to right and left, ten deep behind him and in front. There was only one Old Folk's Home. He drew his shoulders back and inhaled deeply, the tension in his neck slipping off him like a discarded Christmas present and he set off, eager for the coming spring.

The Tailor's Dummy

Nigel Knowles

Well, I don't know why he did it really, but I always thought he was stupid anyway. Besides which, I thought he was joking . . . well, the first time he said it, I did. But I noticed he used to say it on average about once or twice a year.

Then, of course, as we grew older, it got more regular. He actually asked me to arrange it. Arrange it! 'You must be joking,' I said, and forgot all about it until he died.

Then I read the will and his instructions that he had put under the clock on the sideboard. I threw them onto the fire, but, of course, he had given them to the solicitor as well, and so I got a copy in the post the day after.

Seemed strange really . . . well it would have done to outsiders, but I suppose I had got used to the idea over the years.

Very strange instructions indeed, the solicitor said. He was right. I didn't know where to start, so I looked up 'Taxidermist' in the Yellow Pages. I found one under the heading of 'Preservatives and Wood Treatments'. Their name was Grimley, rather apt, I thought.

Anyway, they agreed to do the job and came round straight away. Time was of the essence, Mr Grimley said.

I let them get on with it. They took him to the Parlour and I didn't see him again until the Friday. He looked stupid when I saw him. He'd got a kind of silly grin which made him look peculiar. His cheeks were red, but his ears were very white. My God, I thought, you look awful, look at your hair! It looks like a wig. His teeth looked false and he always used to look after his teeth.

But it was his hands that I disliked the most. Disgusting I thought they were. Ugh! It makes me go goose-pimply every time I think of them. Sort of yellowy, they were, and his nails had been scrubbed with a Brillo pad – really unnatural.

Well, it's all over now, I said to him. No more headaches, no more television, no chocolate, no kippers and no sex.

He looked at me as if to say he didn't care. Neither did I, really.

Anyway, the next part was the hardest. I didn't know how to go about it. I suppose I was embarrassed. In the end, I just walked into the shop and asked to speak to the Manager. You should have seen his face! He agreed to do it on condition that if the Council threatened to close him down, he would have to go. It suited me.

The first day coincided with the Summer Sales. You should have seen the bargain hunters of Kidderminster on that day. They thought, you see, that it was all a big joke . . . part of the publicity to attract the customers.

The Tailor's Dummy looks real, they said. Little children used to climb into the window to touch him. He made some of them cry when they felt his hands. Mind you, I will say this, Grimleys did a good job.

He looked just the same at the end of the Sales as he had on the first day. But he still had that silly grin.

I'd almost forgotten about him when I received the first letter from the shop. Regional Management had taken a very dim view – he would have to come out.

Oh dear, I thought, what can I do with him now? I ignored the letter, but the next one came direct from Regional Management, seven days' notice – they needed the space for their Christmas Grotto.

I had a chat with the Local Manager, his hands were tied, he said. I suggested sending him down to Head Office with their internal delivery service, but he said 'No'.

Well – six months was a long time, I suppose. I strung it out until after the January Sales, but in the end Grimleys brought him home.

Look, there he is now, standing in his favourite place by the window, looking down the street.

I must say, I get a few funny looks from the neighbours sometimes, and the children put their noses right up against the glass and stare at him for ages until they are called away.

I'm not taking him on holiday with me. He can stay here on his own till I get back. Do him good to be on his own for a change anyway after the shop window experience.

Wonder what he's thinking about? He still owes money for the club. I'm not paying it.

It was his birthday last week. I didn't bother with a present, but I made him a nice cup of tea and bought some custard creams. They were his favourite.

I don't know, I looked at him yesterday and I thought he had put a bit of weight on. He looks quite well actually, a lot better than before he died. Well, it's all the fresh air he's been having. I put him outside in the garden when the weather's nice. He likes that. Bloody cats keep sitting on him though. Still, he never complains. He used to complain when he was – you know, with us. Not now though, seems to accept anything I give him. And this is funny, he always used to moan about me smoking. Now, I leave dog-ends everywhere and blow smoke clouds right next to him and he never says a word.

I've started inviting people round, just a few friends and neighbours mostly, although his nephew dropped in and asked if he wanted to go up to the allotment. I told him he wasn't feeling too good and he'd promised to stay indoors to help with the ironing.

The woman next door tends to stare at him rather a lot, which I think is quite rude. It is rude to stare, isn't it, particularly when people are feeling off-colour?

I thought about taking him shopping with me. I bought a wheelchair but he's very heavy.

Must cut down on the custard creams, pet, he used to say, they go straight to my tummy.

I think he's happy. He still has that silly grin on his face, but his cheeks have gone a bit puffy. Filled out a bit, you might say. I don't know why.

He used to get into terrible tempers sometimes, especially if the gas bills were too high or the telephone. He nearly used to explode. Said if I wanted to talk to people, why didn't I catch a bus and go and see them? Doesn't ever mention the phone now, just seems to stare out of the window. But I can feel his eyes everywhere . . . the way he used to pretend to be reading the newspaper but you knew his eyes were everywhere.

He's packed up a few of his bad habits, like breaking

wind when we were watching television, and cleaning out his ears in bed.

Unfortunately, I've noticed that he's picked up a few more recently. I ask you, who wouldn't have something to say about someone who looks so indignant when he's spoken to sometimes. Oh, if looks could kill! There's almost a resentment there. I can tell from his face something seems to be bothering him. I told him straight that if he didn't buck up, I'd send him back to Grimleys. You should have seen the look on his face. It made him sit up and take notice, I can tell you.

He's been very perky since then. Like a new man. He wanted to go out again, so I made the effort, got him into the wheelchair and off we went.

It was murder trying to get him away from people in the Co-Op. That man from the estate asked him for his club money, and the woman from the Community Centre sold him a book of raffle tickets for the Easter Bazaar. I had to pay for them, mind you, he was always pretty mean with his money. We got stuck at the cash till on the way out, and caused a bit of a hold up. The nice man from the cigarette counter got him out by going down like he was in a rugby scrum and pushing the chair through the turnstile.

We went home after that and I made him a nice pot of tea. He didn't win the raffle. The club man called round again, so I paid him up and said we wouldn't be bothering any more.

They sent a glossy magazine from Grimleys. Apparently, at about this time, the dearly-departed, as Grimleys call them, can benefit tremendously from their comprehensive beautification treatment. I looked over at him and read on. Your loved one returned as near to life as it is possible to get. Well . . . in his case, it could have been an improvement.

I decided I'd have a go. I'd been saving the money I would have spent on his little extras and so I thought I would give it a try.

Grimleys collected him on Tuesday, and on Saturday he was back. What a waste of money! I wish I hadn't bothered. He looks sort of, well, I don't know, sort of wicked somehow . . . as if someone had taken a twenty-pound note off him and put a woopsy in his pocket. He hardly speaks at all now. I find it increasingly difficult to have a proper conversation with him. He's boring actually, but I expect he's got his reasons. He was a very stubborn man. Wouldn't give an inch, and used to row with next door all the time about their radio being too loud. I told him, live and let live, but no! Complained to everybody – police, environmental health, the newspapers, but now, not a word. I expect they're very pleased next door, but the strange thing is, not long after he went, they stopped playing the radio.

He used to be a bit colour prejudiced, but look at him now! Old Snow Face, I call him. His skin seems to be going oily, but it's not soft any more. A bit like leather, I'd say.

I went to the zoo the other day and spent ages looking at an alligator. It's him, I thought, in a few years' time, that will be him! I have to laugh, especially if there's something on the telly he doesn't like. Can't do a damn thing about it, can you, I say?

I comb his hair every day. Some of it has come out in the comb. He's losing his hair, isn't he, someone will say? Yes, I say, he's getting old now, it won't be long before he's bald.

Various parts of his anatomy have started to shrink and shrivel up. I won't go into detail, but I think you can imagine.

I got him some new shoes. He's a size eight now, used to be nine. It was when I changed his underpants that I noticed he was smaller. Shrinkage is quite normal at this stage, said Mr Grimley.

It's all a bit odd. It's been over a year now. He's still on the electoral register and he won a holiday in a competition. It was me, of course, but I put it in his name to make him feel wanted. A holiday for two in Torquay – it sounds very nice, but I shan't take him. I'll go with that nice man I met at the Tea Dance. You never know, if we make a go of it, I might divorce Old Snow Face. Mind you, he's company, I suppose, and he doesn't make any demands. That's something in his favour. But I wish just occasionally, he would indulge in one or two of his old bad habits. Just for old time's sake. He used to twist the tablecloth when he was waiting for his pudding. It annoyed me at the time, but I wish he would do it now.

He likes me to leave the television on when I go out. I always say – shan't be long, I'll leave the telly on. Doesn't like being left on his own. Never used to bother before, I could have left him for weeks and he wouldn't have bothered. As long as he had his pipe and his paper, he would sit for hours. When I got back he used to say, a cup of tea would be nice.

Just for a bit of fun, I play the home video of him and me that his nephew did when we were in the garden. It's funny to see him lifting the onions and shouting, look at these, they're the pick of the bunch.

True to form, he did actually swear on the video film as

well, sod it, he said, when he cut his finger opening a can of peaches in the kitchen.

We kissed each other and he gave me a flower from the garden. Happy days really.

His lips are very tough now and going dark. I just kiss him on the cheek when I say goodnight.

He's going quite leathery. I still comb his hair for him, although I don't cut his nails any more. I think they've stopped growing. But on the whole, I will say this, he's kept his figure quite well. He was never fat and could always rely on all of the regular shirt and jacket sizes fitting him. He didn't buy clothes himself, he used to rely on me. I knew the sizes off by heart – nine for shoes, 34 waist and 30 inside leg, 15 collar and hat 6⅞. He used to wear a beret in the garden and those gaiters he kept from the army. I used to say, all you need is a bicycle and you could sell your onions! I won't tell you what he used to say to me. He was always a bit coarse with his language.

It's coming up to his second anniversary. It seems a long time. I really wonder how long I should keep him. Perhaps forty years of marriage was long enough?

I don't see the man at the Tea Dances any more. He slipped a disc doing the Cha Cha Cha. He wanted me to visit him in hospital. I've got enough to do here looking after him.

Had another letter from Grimleys, offering the same service as before. Definitely not bothering this time, he'll have to stay as he is.

I found a letter in one of his jacket pockets the other day. Pity I didn't look before, it would have made my life a lot easier. Apparently, he had been seeing someone else. What a joke – a fancy woman at his age! It had been going on for quite some time. They used to meet in the park and in the pub, because I found another letter underneath an old newspaper in his cupboard. What annoyed me most of all was that she used to come here when I was out.

Bloody cheek!

What they could have found to have got up to at their age is beyond me. I thought, right me lad, I shall take revenge. Well, see how you like being on your own for a bit! I pushed him into the stair cupboard and locked him in. Not that he could have got out I know, but just to teach him a lesson.

Three months he stayed there and he hated it, I could tell. I used to open the door and have a look at him about once a week. Feeling sorry for yourself, my lad, I used to ask. Well, good job too, and so you should.

I had another letter from Grimleys, but I wasn't in any mood to consider having him done up again, so I threw it away without opening it.

It was three months to the day when I let him out of the cupboard. I wheeled him back into the lounge. Well then, my lad, I said, I hope you have learned your lesson? No more fooling about for you!

His nephew called again and asked if he wanted to go up to the allotments. I told him he was suffering from a stomach upset and he would never make it to the toilet if he was taken short.

His nephew looked around the door at him and agreed with me that it was best to leave him where he was.

Oh, I forgot to mention . . . not only did I lock him in the cupboard, I knocked his whatsit off as well. I tapped it with a toffee hammer and it fell off. That's just to make sure there is no more hanky-panky, I told him. You should have seen his face!

His third anniversary was not long after I released him from the cupboard.

The letter from Grimleys arrived by the second post. I decided I would have the special rejuvenation treatment to cheer us both up. Suppose I'm too soft with him really, but, well, we're only on the earth once, aren't we?

Grimleys took him on Tuesday, just like before, and brought him back on the Friday morning. Two hundred pounds it cost me! Not a bad job actually. His face is pinker and there's a twinkle in his eye, but unfortunately his skin is still rather leathery. He definitely looks heavier. His nephew agreed. I can't imagine what Grimleys get up to, but there you are, they know what they're doing, I suppose.

They have this sanctuary called the Garden of Sweet Repose. Actually, it's more like an underground mauso-leum, but they've got a few potted plants and some ivy and it looks quite nice. I must say, the idea quite appeals.

I've started going to the Tea Dances again. I never mention it to him, mind you, it would only make him jealous, I know just what he's like.

I've met a nice man who used to be a market gardener, and I invited him round for tea. He commented on the other person in the room, who, as usual, was sitting in his chair. I told him it was merely a very life-like dummy which I kept for sentimental reasons.

He brings me cabbage and potatoes, beans and lettuce, and someone that I know is very jealous.

I showed my new friend the video of us in our garden. Good onions, he said, but why did he wear that beret?

I've arranged for him to go to the Garden of Sweet Repose. I shan't bother to divorce him now officially, but I think he knows I've done my duty, especially after that other affair.

Grimleys were due to collect him first thing Monday morning. I got up especially early to go over a few things with him and to say a proper goodbye.

Sad really, but there it is. I told him I still loved him, well he wasn't to know any different, and I put a nice flower buttonhole in his jacket. It was a rose actually, they were his favourite.

Grimleys came. They were very discreet, I must say, and took him off in an unmarked car beneath a beautiful floral blanket. It could have been the furniture removal people for all the neighbours knew.

I had a phone call from Mr Grimley. He said he didn't like to mention it, but his whatsit was missing. I told Mr Grimley that it had fallen off when I was changing his trousers. He seemed to accept it.

I go to see him every Tuesday. He's lying down on a bed of marble surrounded by ivy and some aspidistras. I told him that he only needed a few onions and he'd be in seventh heaven. He just smiled the way he used to, but I shed a tear about him, going home on the bus.

Mr Grimley thinks I'm wonderful for bothering with him, but I told him that forty years was a long time.

My friend, the market gardener, passed away, so I'm on my own again. It doesn't bother me. I'll have to start going to the Tea Dances again.

On the other hand, perhaps I might emigrate. It's never too late, they say. I fancy Australia, and Fiji sounds nice. He asked me not to go, but I'm keeping him guessing. I might not, but if I ever found any more of those letters, I'd be off like a shot.

I took his nephew to see him, but he thought it was very morbid. Oh Aunty, he said, why don't you just get rid of him? I gave him all of the gardening equipment – forks, spade, hoe, even his barrow. I'll keep the beret and his gaiters, though.

I still play the video sometimes, when I'm fed up with the television. He still lifts the onions up, pick of the bunch, he says. Then he gives me a kiss and a flower from the garden. I know it all off by heart, and occasionally I feel like telling him, mind that can of peaches, you'll cut yourself! Silly really, I know.

His nephew hardly ever comes round now. It was always him he liked really, I was just here when he came. Never mind, he still uses the tools in the allotment. I've seen him there when I go past on the bus. I give him a wave but he doesn't always see me. It sounds funny, but when I went to Grimleys last time, I didn't bother with any flowers. I took a nice, lovely big ring of onions and put them between the ivy and the aspidistra.

He looks really peaceful lying there between all that vegetation. You've got it made, I say to him. He looks up at me, and do you know what he says? He says, I'm in seventh heaven, here love, I'm in seventh heaven!

For Better, For Worse

Kim Fitzpatrick

Mollie Turnbull had grown embittered in the two years the old house had been up for sale. It seemed nobody would give good money for a neglected farmhouse with a closed-down butcher's shop tacked onto its side.

She was seventy-three now, and two years of her precious life had been wasted in suspension. And for what? She'd never get a bungalow at this rate! It was Mat's fault. He should have sold up while he'd still had the energy to forge a new life. Her anger seethed and frothed, giving her acid indigestion, and bringing back long-forgotten memories of cider-making in the barn. Everything was memory now. Her role in life had spent itself along with Mat's decreasing energies. He had to shut the shop five years ago – there was no longer a demand for rural butchers. Then the pigs had had to go, then the land, and one by one the boys had all got married, scattered now, the length and breadth of England . . . There was only her left, and this frail old man who would not eat. She bristled. He'd be in soon for his coffee and biscuits. The old fool would *not* wear his dentures and eat proper food, no matter how she nagged.

'I can't bear the discomfort,' he said, 'they chafe me.' They were still in their box in the bathroom. But he'd never been able to cope with change. He'd held her back at every turn. Stopped her selling the place when all was in working order, and the interest rate was low, insisting on carrying on to the bitter end until he was worn out, self-pitying, neglectful. No thought for her. But she knew as soon as she saw him dipping his ginger nuts into his coffee that pity would overtake her anger. He would slurp them around his empty old mouth trying to nourish himself with the pulp, his hand on the cup strangely fragile . . . artist's hands, in another life. She found it difficult to remember them in their happy, active days; killing pigs, swilling out with iron buckets, butchering massive carcasses of beef. She knelt on the cold hearthstone, bad-temperedly sweeping ashes into her shovel, as she had for fifty years, remembering with doubtful hope that people were coming to view. They wouldn't buy . . . Nobody with any sense would want this place.

She stopped sweeping for a moment, and sat back thinking wistfully of the gas logs she'd have if she ever got a bungalow. They were quite realistic now, flickered like real ones so that you got shadows on the wall. Then she pictured the bathroom; avocado suite, mirror tiles, and a crinoline lady round the toilet roll. She'd have a patio too, a little table and a sun-shade . . . tea on a tray in the sun . . .

She could no longer kindle any sentiment for the old house. Her impatience to leave had exposed a yearning for cheap modernity, and the feminine things she'd been denied . . .

'It'd look ridiculous in here, Mother . . . Save your money.'

'You'll have to wait, Moll, we need a couple of new pigsties first . . .'

Sometimes, she'd admitted, secretly, that the little knick-knacks, as the boys called them, would look out of place, or worse, be knocked over by her clumsy menfolk ill-at-ease among such things, but it had not stopped her wanting them.

She stacked the grate with wood, laying the smallest bits at the bottom; poking scraps of newspaper between the cracks, planning to light it when Mat came through for he felt the cold these days. He was in the empty shop again, avoiding her, and trying to recapture his happy working life. He'd be sitting in the window-seat reading the old account books and making phone calls to business people who could no longer be bothered with him.

She had seen how he did it; taking a deep breath as he dialled in an effort to summon up his old authority before demanding the market price of pigs and the exact time of the auction. She pitied him when his voice faltered and grew weak as he persisted with his pointless enquiries. She imagined one of the new breed of college-trained young market men on the other end of the line; his mocking impatient eyes on the ceiling, cursing this old fool who wasted time still ringing in when he had no business now . . .

She heard him replacing the receiver, the single tinkle echoing round the stone-cold shop, bouncing off the counter and the dusty, flagged floor, feeling the empty silence as he must feel it, and wishing that things were different.

He was only an echo of the Mat she'd married. She would often catch herself remembering him as he used to be, looking at the kitchen door through which she half-expected him to come striding – coming in to wash after killing a pig for the shop, or after mowing one of the meadows. Straight-up he'd been with fingers thickened by hard masculine work – swollen sometimes . . . Rough on her skin. She drew back from expanding on that, not wanting to recall their sexual life . . . just something else she'd had to put up with. Instead, she saw him swilling his big arms at the kitchen sink, changing from bloody overalls into sweetly-starched white coat, and striped apron. She saw him behind a mound of steaming potatoes, and three or four pork chops.

He limped in from the shop, his hernia truss askew, knobbly under his trousers, pathetically trying to be what he once was; hearty, amiable. He would never admit to growing old, or that his role in life was finished. She wondered if he heard his own voice tremble, or saw his bent back. Perhaps not minding that too much . . . seeing echoes of his younger self; a successful man, carrying burdens, a side of beef, the responsibilities of a butcher-farmer.

She went on sitting by the old curved hearthstone, her dismay turning to anger again for she knew she could help him if he let her. She wanted to shout at him; tell him to keep out of the shop, look forward for a change, get his dentures in and eat the food she cooked, but she knew he wouldn't, and with that knowledge so her own role passed.

'We've been here fifty years, Mother, I think we ought to see it through. Bungalows aren't for the likes of us.'

She had hated him when he'd said that, but the resignation in his croaky voice had made her swallow her anger, and she'd continued to bide her time. She knew that he saw no life for himself away from the old place and she understood. Perhaps there wouldn't be, but it was her turn now, and she would not give way to him. She was still strong and had desires whereas he was fading away fast. She prayed each night for somebody to buy the house quickly now, beseeching God to ignore Mat's prayers for them to stay.

He lowered himself into his chair, relying on his stick for support. His lips were blue so she struck a match and put it to the fire, knowing exactly where the little flame should go, the twigs and paper swooshing into light and heat.

Silently, she cursed him for ageing quicker than herself. He had used himself up without any thought for the renewal she had planned for them both.

She rounded on him. 'You bin in that cold shop again all mornin', Dad?'

She was inarticulate, unable to communicate the bitterness that had overtaken her. She wanted to hurt him now she was no longer afraid of him, as he had once hurt her.

'I think I'll have a couple o' ginger-nuts this mornin', Mother,' he said. He was sly now his assertiveness had gone, and feeling her anger, shut her out with his eyelids, lowering his chin onto his chest as if for a nap, knowing she would leave him in peace and go and make his coffee.

It was a perverse way of comforting herself to recall the many evenings he had left her when she had been young and pretty with the blocks to scrub, the boys to bathe and put to bed. Off he had driven, on tenterhooks and spinning tyres to fatstock dinners, masonic lodges, bowling clubs and skittles matches, ambitious in clean, white shirts, anxious for self-improvement.

She remembered the lonely days she had spent minding the shop while he had charmingly hawked his meat from his Morris van, haphazardly filling it up each morning, uncaring in his zest to be off, leaving her without knives, or any of the good stuff, so that sometimes all she could offer her customers was stewing-meat and offal.

She'd been frightened of him then, when she was timid, but she'd known that, in a different way and unadmitted, he was afraid too; of being put-down, or thought a fool, and in self-protection he had raised his voice and bellowed like a tethered bull, defying anybody to take him on. Yet underlying all this had been a bluff good humour and a crude quick wit that had endeared him to people.

But his rages had scarred her, fifty years on and she could still remember the day she'd mistakenly sold Miss Pringle a fillet of beef instead of chuck-steak. Not realising its worth she had taken it into her kitchen to hack it up with the breadknife, afterwards innocently bolstered up by the old girl's rare praise and false humour.

He was furious when he'd found the fillet gone, having promised it to Colonel Maunder.

'Don't you know yet, woman,' he'd bellowed, 'that there's only one fillet in each beast! It's the prime cut. You got threepence for something worth five bob!'

She had known there was more to it than that; he always saved the best for the Colonel, taking it down in the evenings when he'd washed, shaved, and put on his suit. Wrapping up the meat with a sprig of parsley and a couple of onions he had driven down the village like a divine benefactor, to be invited in for whisky and dirty jokes.

They were two of a kind, Colonel Maunder and Mat Turnbull, everybody said.

He had sulked for days, a missed opportunity to get his foot in the door of a village bigwig. To add insult to injury, Miss Pringle had waved his van down the next day, proffering another threepenny bit, 'for some more of that beautifully tender chuck-steak.'

She watched their car drive into the yard, despairing as the pot-holes spattered it with mud. She had feared they would not come for it was threatening to snow, and twice she had gone out to see how the house would appear to them. Standing low in the middle of its remaining half acre she had noticed for the first time in years how the roof sagged, and how unbalanced it looked with the end chimney-pot missing. The windows looked dismal too, little squares of black reflecting the winter sky, and wet black polythene flapped from the doorless frames of the empty pigsties. It depressed her, and she understood why nobody wanted to buy.

She remembered it in its hey-day – the rancid-sweet smell of pigs that had hung in the air, friendly wet snouts poking comically under the doors of the sties. She caught the echoes of rattling buckets, the whistling of her sons as they swept and swilled, seeing their young, powerful bodies lifting fresh straw. She saw the boats they'd always made from their sweet wrappers sailing in the trough, and Patch barking, calling her in to tend the shop . . .

The couple came up the path, and she sighed at their youth. But as she opened the door the lad was speaking and with his words Mollie's heart soared as high as it ever had.

'I'd give up all my prospects in the company for this place, Carol. Start where the old ones leave off, forget materialism, live plainly, like these people have . . .'

She gave them tea by the fire, throwing on logs with abandon, knowing how well her old furniture reflected the flames. She felt them respond, felt the tranquillity soothing their modern stress.

'Sold!' she said to herself, her heart glowing like the old room she had completely rejected. The bungalow's flower-papered sitting-room slipped into mind, and she saw it filled with little shelves on which sat miniature glass animals, china vases, and onyx ashtrays.

'It's like tearing ivy off a wall for me to leave here, Mother.' Mat, reluctant to the end, watched her pack.

The bungalow was all she had dreamed of. She resurrected her childhood to play doll's houses again but when the autumn came she was reminded of the old house, and wanted Mat to take her back.

It looked well, as it always had in late September, the stone as mellow and golden as the afternoon. The windows winked in the sun, newly-shone and newly-clad in bright yellow cloth. The young man sat on the roof hammering the tiles with firm, strong strokes, a new chimney-pot awaiting him.

'I ought to have done that, Mother.' Mat's voice,

stronger now was full of resentment. 'If I hadn't neglected the old place we'd still be here.'

She held her tongue. She had known he would forget his new-found contentment and be jealous of any restoration. He had fought change tooth and nail and now regretted it. She shrugged, complacent now her own struggles were over.

The girl, pale and quiet, was clad in a plastic apron peeling apples. She stood a long way from the old sink as if distancing herself from her chore. Apples filled the room, spilling out into the garden, score upon score, awaiting her tiny peeler. And the plums still to be picked . . .

Mollie saw her brave attempts; the old lace cloth on the table, the fire laid ready to light, but she also recognised the girl's misgivings. Dejection curved her back and, unchecked, her curly hair had grown into heavy ringlets. Mollie wasn't surprised. This old-fashioned, compliant girl was trying to please her man. He had rejected the modern world, spurning progress, insisting on the old exhausting methods; trying to recreate a way of life that had long since passed. Mollie knew what they were trying to achieve, but wanted to show the girl the electric peeling-machine in her mail-order catalogue, suggest she buy it, as she would if she were young again.

The husband came in and Mollie thought how he had changed too. Confident, domineering now, like Mat at his age. And Mollie left them wondering if the girl ever dreamed of gas logs and bungalows.

The Book Reviver

Graham Marsden

There was no need to eject me. No need to send for the police. But they did. One of the policemen looked like a professional footballer. Pink skin. A ridge of fat between cheek-bone and eye-socket – slightly more on the left side. When he pretended to smile the fat wrinkled on the left but not on the right. The other one, the one who hung back, was round-shouldered and thin. His helmet was too big. My pals looked on. They could do no more. One day I shall return.

They're a good crowd. My Central Library pals. I limit the encomium to those who frequent Floor One. The Arts floor. Seldom having alighted at other floors, my knowledge of their regulars is too flimsy to support a judgment. An opinion yes but nothing more. I once visited the Science, Politics and Business Studies floor but didn't like the atmosphere. Abrasive. We never speak to each other, my pals and I on the Arts floor. Although many ignore the convention, we know you shouldn't speak in libraries, so we don't. I rarely speak at all these days and my pals respect that. We exchange nods and smiles. First to reach his place is 'Stocky'. 'Stocky' is my private name for him. In my head. He wears a brownish overcoat and has grey stubble on his chin. Along the side wall of the Arts floor is a line of luxuriously comfortable study-cubicles each with a chair and a writing shelf under a window. 'Stocky' favours the second cubicle from the end closest to the oversize art books. As soon as the doors open at nine-thirty he heads for his cubicle, sits down, reaches across the gangway and takes two art books from the nearest shelf. He opens them at random and pretends to make notes on a sheet of paper. Inside ten minutes he's asleep. 'Stocky' is a scholar and to see him select two books is a relief. Another scholar taught me that to purloin information from one book is plagiarism but to take from two is scholarship. In the first cubicle at the other end most mornings 'Punter' studies his racing reference books. At lunchtime 'Punter' leaves. I think he attends the bookmakers. There are other regulars, each distinguished in his or her own way. In the fiction section 'Milly' goes through the paperbacks with the speed of a bank-clerk counting fivers. Living disproof of the legend 'you can't judge a book by its cover', 'Milly' holds court three times a week.

One thing about the regulars is that none of them, ever, would deface a library book with pencil marks. I despise library-book defacers. We suffer an excess of book deface-ment on the Arts floor and whenever I find a book with passages underlined and marginal comments in pencil and sometimes even in ink I become angry. I seethe. Three months ago I decided that seething was a sterile response. From Sainsburys I bought a large soft green rubber eraser; beautiful and pliant. Now, whenever I find a defaced book on the shelves I take it to a spare cubicle and rub out the pencil marks as best I can. Often the vandal has pressed on hard and much as I try I cannot entirely revive it. What sort of people deface library books? They cannot be book-lovers. For some fleeting expedient of their own they are willing to impede the studies of others. In particular I cannot understand it on the Arts floor. The Science, Politics and Business Studies floor, yes. During my visit to that floor I inspected some of the books. I didn't like them. Nothing but people's tedious opinions about trivia. No beauty. I can understand students underlining passages in these books. Perhaps to record their disagreement. Or to enshrine a passage in their minds in order to pass off the opinion as their own in some examination or essay or suchlike. Most of the paragraphs would need some such retrieval cue; they would scarcely be memorable without. The readers on the Science, Politics and Business Studies floor gave off an aura of greed. Interested only in them-selves and displaying no love of books. And the books all seemed to have been written by kindred spirits of the readers. Were I required by circumstances to read many books on that floor I might be forced to deface a few myself. That's some measure of the distaste I felt.

When I revive a maimed book I do so surreptitiously. I position the book carefully on the inside edge of the writing shelf and turn my shoulder outwards so my rubbing out cannot be seen. The doing of good works should be a clandestine activity carried out for its own sake. 'You cannot achieve a state of grace through good works,' my grandmother would say. 'God will see through you and recognise you for a schemer.' So I never drew attention to the hours I spent in the Library rubbing out pencil marks in books. I sought no praise. I merely wished to be left alone. To seek attention would inevitably draw me towards conversation with a member of staff. And as I no longer speak this would be difficult and unnerving for them. Although I no longer speak my hearing is good. Too good. People chatter; chatter chatter chatter all the time. Even on the Arts floor. I know, and my pals know, that talking in libraries is against the law. But when the two policemen arrived people went on talking and neither of the officers reproached them. I thought they would but they didn't. In a letter to Barbara Pym, Philip Larkin reported his hearing-aid broken – but decided to leave it unrepaired for a week or so. To lose one's hearing for a while. Ah, yes. Since Anna died I have grown my hair long and allowed it to thicken over my ears. This reduces the noise a little but not much and I am hoping the thicker the mat the more efficient the sound-proofing qualities.

I have also stopped shaving and now have the full beard God intended for me. Each day, as it grows, the closer I grow to God. When Anna died I resolved to shave no more. For the past forty years I had shaved hair from my face in order to simulate the facial characteristics of a woman. It pleased Anna so I did it. Willingly. But the rigmarole of shaving such a ragabash. And so expensive. Simply by not shaving I save on razor-blades, shaving-soap, the wear and tear on towels, and hot water. Not that I have hot water in my room but my savings will last a little while longer and I have more free time to walk, to read and to think. My savings. Ah, yes. I bet that's surprised you. To learn of my savings. After Anna's funeral the solicitor said, 'Make no decisions for six months.'

I made none. I didn't go out. The milkman left milk

each day, and bread and eggs once a week, with a bill. I had enough to pay the bill for three months. Then I went to the Building Society and withdrew more money. I didn't have to say anything. I took the Building Society book with me, filled in a withdrawal slip at the counter and the girl gave me cash. While out I visited the new Sainsburys round the corner for the first time. I stocked up on tinned fruit, soup and whisky to replenish Anna's store cupboard. I burned letters as they arrived. Obviously I was already listed on many computers. People from work came and knocked on the door. Several times. I stood at the window to reassure them as to my health. But I said nothing. They stopped coming. At the end of the six months I wrote to the solicitor and instructed him to sell everything. The house and all the contents, I said, take out money to meet your bill, and pay the residue into the Building Society. Then I left the house and found a room to rent.

Each Monday, Wednesday and Friday, barring Bank Holidays, I withdraw a few pounds from the Building Society. I am not required to speak. My landlady is kind and never requires me to speak. Each Friday I post a small plastic bag containing my rent-book and exact money through her letter-box. Each Saturday morning she slides the plastic bag containing the rent-book under my door. She initials the payments. When I first occupied my room she advised me to go the 'Social' because they would give me money. The boy behind the counter insisted on my address. I didn't want him to have it. He wanted to list it on a computer and people would know where I live and might visit me and require me to speak. I didn't want that. Whenever I go to the Library or to Sainsburys I follow a circuitous route down a ginnel which leads to the disused railway sheds. Sometimes I go one way through them, sometimes another. My landlady is kind and does not mind that I go out of the back door sometimes instead of the front. At the rear gate I sometimes turn right, sometimes left. A determined person could trace me, I know that but I will not make it easy.

At Sainsburys I am not required to speak. I collect my purchases in a wire basket. The check-out girl passes them over a magic eye which adds up the prices. Green figures describe a total in a window like a letter-box between us. I pay the amount due. The girl is black and kind and pretty. Often she smiles at me and laughs. She never requires me to speak. I always attend her till even if there's a queue, which annoys the Security Guard. Once when she was away I attended another till and a middle-aged haughty woman asked questions of me. When I declined to answer she became angry and I had to abandon my purchases at the counter. I ate bread unbuttered for a week and drank no whisky. At no extra charge the girl in Sainsburys gives me a plastic bag in which to carry my purchases. I don't know whether or not I am supposed to but I use the bag for the rest of the week to carry the things I need while I'm out. In my black overcoat I have one good pocket in which I carry my quarter-bottle of whisky. Nothing is more pleasant than sitting in the fresh air to enjoy a few sips of whisky during the day. I particularly like the Market Square where I can watch people walking. Each day I refill the small bottle from my larger weekly bottle. My other pockets, my trouser pockets, are worn through and loose change, my rubber eraser, and my pencil would soon be lost. So I carry these items, together with a little bread, in my Sainsburys bag. I save the plastic bags in my room. The bags are perfectly sound. I might be asked for them back, or Sainsburys could stop providing them, so now I have a good-sized stockpile put by. 'Waste not, want not,' as my grandmother would say.

When the policemen arrived at the Library I decided not to speak to them. You are not required to. Three times a week when I have drawn money from the Building Society I go to the Newmarket public-house. The licensee is kind and never tries to engage me in conversation. The girl in the Building Society provides plenty of loose change in my money and I can usually place the exact price of a pint of beer on the public-house counter. From the television in the pub I know you don't have to speak to the police. Many times I have seen officers on the television say to people, 'You are not obliged to say anything.' A considerate touch. I wish everybody thought the same. If you are wondering why I no longer speak I will tell you. I don't speak because when people see me they lower their voices and turn their heads towards each other. I have simply lowered my voice so far that I now remain silent. On the television a police officer accused a man of crimes and told him that he need not say anything. The accused said, 'I have nothing to say.' Yes and No. There are many things I wish to say but I do not wish to speak.

When I first started attending the Library I was still speaking. I wanted to join and to have tickets but the librarian insisted on my address – in writing. I would not give it. She wanted to list me on her computer. So now I read in the Library itself between nine-thirty in the morning and eight in the evening. I never read the newspapers in the Library although many do. I do not wish to learn the contents. If anything sufficiently important happens I will hear discussion of it in the pub. But I enjoy the crossword puzzles on the backs of newspapers. I solve them in my head. Occasionally I mark in an answer with my pencil – to fix the other clues in my head. But mostly not. The little bin at the railway station supplies an excellent source of newspapers. People buy them to read on the train and on arrival abandon them. The crossword puzzles are rarely completed. I like the railway station. People to watch and comfortable benches to sit on. And near the railway station is the second-hand clothes shop where I bought my welling-ton boots. When Anna died I wore my suede shoes. The rest were sold in the house sale. My suede shoes leaked in the wet weather. One morning en route to the railway station for papers I saw the wellington boots in a cardboard box outside the second-hand shop. A beautiful matt finish – a well cut shape to the foot – stylishly short uppers. As I lifted them up from the other footwear in the box the shop-owner emerged from his door.

'A pound to you, friend,' he said, 'there's years of wear left in them wellingtons.'

I stood with them in my hands and pondered. I sensed he was a truthful man.

'What size do you take?' he asked.

I did not wish to speak but I desperately wanted the boots.

'I can get in anything above a nine,' I muttered. He laughed.

'They'll do you a treat then,' he said and held out his hand. I paid him a pound coin and put them on. My wellington boots confer flexibility and freedom from decision-making. Waterproof in all weathers and no need for boot-polish. Dust dirties them, the rain cleans them.

The Lord giveth and the Lord taketh away. And no need for socks. Socks need to be washed and mended or replaced. Another waste of time and money. In my room the wellingtons are as comfortable as the slippers Anna would buy me for Christmas. When outdoors I stuff my trousers in the tops of my wellingtons to prevent the trouser bottoms from becoming scuffed. My trousers are fashionably torn at the knees. One day I noticed that young people nowadays wear their jeans torn at the knee so I tore my trousers. I do not wish to be thought old-fashioned. I have three good shirts – all the same – not quite check, but blue and green lines cross a white background. They give me great pleasure. Anna bought them for me from a mail-order firm in the old days.

When the police arrived at the Arts floor the fat-faced one said, 'Libraries are no place for louts and lay-abouts.'

Although I agreed, I said nothing. Instead I pointed to the young lout who had defaced the book. He sat at the table with another book in front of him. Grinning. Ten minutes earlier, rounding the corner of twentieth-century English poetry, I had seen him, actually seen him, underlining a passage in pencil. Approaching the corner of the table I pointed to the passage. He ignored me. I tapped on the table with the quarter-bottle of whisky from my pocket. He looked up. On the table in front of the book lay his tin pencil-box which simulated a large bar of Cadbury's Dairy Milk Chocolate. I opened it to look for his rubber eraser. He grabbed the pencil-box and the contents spilled onto the table. As I suspected – no rubber eraser. The chattering on the Arts floor stopped. He left the book and ran to the enquiry desk. I carried the book to a cubicle, took my own rubber eraser from my Sainsburys bag, turned my shoulder on the kibbitzers and began to remove the offending marks.

The thin policeman whose helmet was too big said, 'Come on, Pop – we don't want any trouble.'

I moved to sit at the central table expecting to make a written statement about the young vandal. I did not wish to speak. On the television in the pub I have often seen police officers say to people, 'Do you wish to make a written statement?' But this is not what the policemen wanted. The fat-faced one seized my shoulder and said, 'Out. Right now.'

The one with the over-sized helmet hung back. I stood erect, picked up my Sainsburys bag, and walked towards the door. My pals looked sympathetic but said nothing. I am glad they did not, the policemen would have been angry with them too, needlessly.

'And don't let me catch you in here again,' said the fat-faced one.

Without wishing to sound waspish I must tell you I had received no impression of him spending much time in libraries, so a chance meeting would have been unlikely. But I concurred with his general drift. It seemed that the Library, Arts floor at least, does not object to people who deface books. Such a place is no place for me. So now, I spend more time in my room. The day I moved in I discovered a treasure, left I thought by the previous occupants. A whole roll of unused wallpaper. A pretty pattern of spring violets and primroses in a tiny buff-coloured basket. Around the handle of the basket curls a garland of ivy leaves. The motif is repeated at intervals and has given me much pleasure. I worried at first lest the previous occupants should want it back. But no one came. After some weeks I knocked on my landlady's door and placed the roll in her hands. She looked perplexed for some seconds but then said, 'No. I don't want it. It was left over when my husband decorated our bedroom. You can keep it.' She smiled and returned it to my hands.

I mean to put it to good use. After the policemen ejected me from the Library I examined the wallpaper carefully. I enjoyed the motif again and the back of the paper is plain; a creamy off-white surface which carries a pencil-mark without smudging. I have cut the roll into long strips. I already have a pencil. It was on my windowsill when I arrived and writes a firm black line without scratching. The pencil is painted yellow and has a pink rubber eraser attached by a small golden cylinder and the wood smells of fir-cones when I sharpen the point. I have seen similar pencils in packs of six at Sainsburys. On my next shopping trip I shall buy a pack and if the previous occupants return to claim their pencil I shall give them a new one in exchange. I have started to write my own book. And no one shall deface it.

In Memory

Henrietta Soames

I am not a person for mementoes. I do not keep anniversaries. I don't know the date she died. I know the month, and only that because it's the same month as I was born. She died two or three weeks before my birthday. A macabre sort of present. I don't know the date. I don't want to know the date.

I don't keep cards, or sprigs of bouquets, or little objects to put on the mantelpiece. My children's drawings are kept by their aunt. I don't have photographs. What good is a dead image if you cannot have the living?

But I have kept her letters.

Today, clearing out my desk I came across them. The whole bundle with her untidy handwriting sprawled so extravagantly over the electric red and blue and green of her writing paper. The words slanting over the pages, written on waves, oscillating, a graph of her emotions. Here were the torn envelopes opened in haste when the contents were still a mystery, a surprise I was eager for. Here were the folds she had made, the mistakes she'd crossed out, the tear at the top of the page she'd turned too hastily. And the handwriting, always difficult to decipher, demanding to be understood, the sentences left unfinished, the thoughts not followed through, the hints, the clues, the nuances I had to read between, suggestions I was expected to pick up on, tests I was expected to pass.

So I came across her letters that, despite myself, I have kept, and I held my hand back from the fire for a moment and thought, these are my only link with her. These letters are my only link.

But of course they are no link. They are a rope trailing in the water, unattached. They are only a proof, I suppose, that she lived. That on those dates scribbled carelessly at the top, she sat down and put marks on these sheets of red and blue and green paper that were her hallmark. But the letters are not living. The phrases are static, the folds made, the love plucked and eaten hungrily long ago. I could learn these letters off by heart and they would still weigh heavy and useless, indigestible, a stone that will not wear away, an address to which it is impossible to reply.

You need the living to catalyse letters, to agitate them into the froth of exchange. You cannot answer back the dead, they always have the last word. Theirs is the triumphant chorus and you sit in the auditorium wanting a final note to resolve the symphony. But the dead leave when they like. They keep their own time. They don't hear your song, they are busy singing their own.

She didn't cry at the funeral because everyone else was. It was too public a place for her tears. She stood on the hassock defying God, defying the Church, defying the priest to make her cry, to break her down into the little pieces that were expected of her. She stood like a pillar between her father and sister, gripping their hands. I will not cry, she thought. I will not cry when they are crying. They need my strength. I will not cry.

When the coffin was carried through she observed it as dispassionately as she would a crate of furniture. That box had nothing to do with her mother. None of the charade had anything to do with her mother. None of it meant anything. None of it was real.

She heard the priest and thought with a bitter smile that if he knew how she'd died he wouldn't be so liberal with his unctuous praises. The Church didn't like – But she couldn't bring the word to the front of her mind because by pronouncing it she would make it real, the molten glass would solidify and crack in the cold air. Like this, it could have been an accident. Her silly old woman was drunk often enough and might not have known . . .

Outside in the spring sunshine (only a couple of weeks or so till her eighteenth birthday) all the flowers were out, roses, lilac, laburnum (the nearest thing to mimosa and she'd made up a bunch of them to put . . .). A helpful little breeze blew away any smoke that might have hovered from the chimney. She stood and comforted the guests. When they came up to give their condolences she apologised to them like a hostess smoothing over a mishap at a party. 'No, really, I'm so sorry. Yes, I'm fine. Please don't be upset. I'm terribly sorry.'

They all came back to the house and stood around awkwardly while she and her sister pressed smoked salmon sandwiches on them that they didn't want to eat. Their father had put photographs on the mantelpiece and these they removed discreetly. They felt that they were in bad taste. They ruined the party.

People's faces change. I probably wouldn't recognise her now but I am reminded. Sometimes a way of walking, or the angle of a chin, a tone of voice or hair swept up into an untidy bun. . . . Sometimes the texture of a fifty-year-old woman's face when the skin loses its elasticity. . . . Sometimes a mother calling her children, a mouth spreading into a smile. . . . The sight of mimosa, the sound of opera. . . . Sometimes, sometimes. . . .

There is a voice that whispers, maybe by the alchemy of these things I will resurrect her. That voice holds onto the letters. It whispers that to destroy them I would be destroying her. I would be betraying the 'love and millions of kisses' she flung onto the end of the page, the 'your silly old woman, your Mamma' that I will never receive from another. The signature I used to try to copy so that I should keep her hand with me always. The fingers of those words that still touch me.

So I have kept them until now. Even though it is heresy, even though it is sentimental, even though it is superstitious. So, I have kept them. Until now.

Immediately after they told her, they wouldn't let her back to the house. She had to stay at a friend's. As soon as she was allowed back she went straight upstairs to the room. Her old woman's room. The room where she had spent most of her time, her weekends, her evenings, her days stolen from school. The room that was always comfortably

messy with clothes and books and records and old newspapers. Half-drunk cups of coffee mouldering by the bed,
empty bottles of vodka peeping out of the bin. The room
that smelt of powder and scent and cigarettes. The room
sprigged with memorabilia, photographs, drawings, old
cuttings of diets and recipes, concert programmes, theatre
tickets. Desiccated mimosa in dry vases, torn stockings,
hidden bars of chocolate, first locks of baby hair. Scarves,
brash t-shirts, silk dresses squashed beneath her old woman
as she sat on the rocking chair doing her make-up and
calling for shoes to be found, coffee to be made, cigarettes
to be lit. The room she and her sister were often paid to
clean up. The room that was only half painted, an experi-
mental pink her old woman was spending some years
getting used to. The room that had dust inches thick on
the picture rail. 'It won't get any higher,' she said. 'I read
it somewhere.' Like Canute she held up her hand to halt
nature and unlike Canute she was obeyed.

To this room she went in search. Like a child looking for
hidden Easter eggs certain there will be some somewhere.
Rushing to find them before anyone else. There'd be a
note, a letter, something, something for her.

But the room was tidy. They'd taken away the vast
horsehair bed she used to sprawl on with her sister,
reading their comics every Saturday, the bed she'd tucked
her mother into when she was drunk. They'd tidied away
all the clothes, the books, the clutter of glasses and plates
and trays. The dressing table was closed up. No bottles of
skin tonic or tubes of anti-wrinkle cream. No lipstick-
stained handkerchieves. The arc of powder had been
swept from the floor. Even the bin was empty. No record
on the gramophone, no bookmark in a book. They'd

tidied her away. Someone had come in and tidied her mother away.

She stood in the centre and thought, this is a strange room, someone else's room. I've never been here before. My old woman has never been here either. My old woman has never been.

It's strange to think that she's never been here. Never seen the house I live in. Never met my husband, my children. They don't think about their grandmother, she doesn't exist for them. Of course one day they'll want to know about her and as I tell them I'll see in their eyes the baffled look that children have when they realise their parents had a life before them. It's a shocking thing to discover, the antecedence of your parents. How could they exist before you? There wasn't any world before you. That they lived without you once is a mystery. That they have had a life that is separate, in which you have been an incident, important, yes, but not crucial, among other incidents, is profoundly disturbing. With all these questions they will look at me while I reach for answers, stretch to the tops of the trees for explanations that will bend a safe reality around them. I will mould certainty into walls to protect them. And they will keep their childhood like a well-known book to dip into and take comfort from. No pages so sharp that they cut themselves. No handwriting they cannot read. No stabbing signatures. No surprises saying, THE END. The book of their childhood will become the book of their adulthood without any sudden division. No clumsy tacking, no join, seamless.

These letters have stitched me to her. Now I am pulling at the thread.

For a long time after, she'd wake in the night and call confusedly for her old woman. She dreamt that it had never happened, that it had all been a horrible joke and there was her mother mocking her for believing it. In the sudden joy of waking she'd think, it's all right, she's back, oh . . .

At Christmas and on her birthday there was always a present missing. Then she stopped looking amongst the parcels but instead into the lucky chances of her own life. Her first job coinciding with her birthday week was one present, meeting her husband at a Christmas party was another. She told no one of these gifts, they were the secrets between herself and her old woman.

So she kept her alive.

But she weighs on me now. She is heavy like a belt pulled tight, a thick belt whose fingers dig into my lungs and squeeze my breath. I feel myself ossifying, petrifying, turning to stone. Lot's wife because she looked back.

And I, who have never kept so much as a lock of the children's hair, I, who will not look at the photograph albums their aunt keeps for them. I, who have been so ruthless with mementoes, am glued to these letters, these insignificant pieces of paper wooing me with their, 'darling', 'sweetheart', 'best beloved . . .'.

We are selling the house. Her house. It's too big for my father to live in alone. He's found a buyer and is moving to a small cottage by the sea. Tomorrow I have to go over and clear all the things away. All the things that have been left there, all the old things. 'They're all to go,' he says. 'I haven't room for them. Take them or throw them away.' There's a big skip ready in the drive.

I could put the letters in a bundle and just throw them in. Or I could scatter them throughout like the raisins in a cake.

It'll be a hard day, a dirty day. From the attic to the cellar we'll be dragging out a decade of memories. Old school reports to laugh over, forgotten crazes to recall. Once-fashionable clothes, a collection of glass animals, maybe even a secret diary of first loves, all coating us with the dust of their memories that for the last time we'll breathe deep into our lungs.

Irritable by the evening, we'll be regretting throwing out so much. But whatever we try tiredly to retrieve will be buried at the bottom of the mound and we'll have to let it go with a shrug.

The letters will be scattered. I'll never find one of them.

'You'll always remember?' her old woman was saying. 'Promise me you'll always remember. The good times, you'll remember the good times, won't you, darling? Promise me.' This said holding her elder daughter's chin and looking hard into her eyes. They were sitting by a lake, it was hot and blue, the water sparkling, their cove, their special place, deserted. Holidays. Just the two daughters and their mother lying in swimsuits by the lake, happy. No rows, no visitors, nothing to put her old woman on edge. No drinking. 'You'll remember the good times?' she pleaded again, and the girl laughed and kissed her and promised, oh, anything, everything, just so that she could see the glow of pleasure return to her mother's face.

Then she ran into the water forgetting everything.

Contributors

WILLIAM BEDFORD lives in Grimsby. He writes full time and his book of poems, *Journeys*, was published by Agenda Editions. He has had stories published in *London Magazine*, *London Review of Books* and *Encounter*. His first novel, *Happiland*, was published recently by William Heinemann.

KIM FITZPATRICK was born in Yorkshire and is of Irish-Scottish descent. She now lives in Dorset and is currently working on a novel.

STEVE GARNER is a full-time English teacher, a part-time writer and a vocalist with an Indie Band. He lives in the Midlands.

DAPHNE GLAZER lives in Hull. Her stories have appeared in several periodicals, including *Critical Quarterly*, *New Statesman*, *Spare Rib*, *Panurge* and *Iron*. She is also the author of a novel, *Three Women*.

LINDA KEMPTON was born in Derby where she still lives. She has recently given up her job as a lecturer to concentrate on writing. She is currently working on a children's novel, while continuing to write short stories.

NIGEL KNOWLES left school with no formal qualifications but after working as a carpet weaver for ten years he obtained a BA Hons degree in Politics. He has recently given up his job as a trade union officer to write plays, stories and novels. He lives in Worcestershire.

PATRICK LAMBE was born in Middlesbrough. He works as a librarian in Birmingham and edits two journals. He has written children's stories and is now planning a novel.

ROSEMARY MACKAY is a native of Aberdeen where she is a part-time tutor with the WEA. Her stories have appeared in various anthologies including *Original Prints* (Polygon Press), *The Edinburgh Review* and *Three's Company* (Keith Murray Publications).

ALAN MAHAR was born in Liverpool but now lives and works in Birmingham, where he is a copywriter for a design and publishing company. His stories have appeared in *London Magazine, Critical Quarterly* and *Bête Noire*.

GRAHAM MARSDEN retired early from the police force as a result of a long-term spinal problem. He now uses his time to write. His ambitions are to have a novel published and to outlive Mrs Thatcher!

WILMA MURRAY was born in rural Aberdeenshire. She is a lecturer at Northern College in Aberdeen. Her stories have appeared in several magazines and anthologies including *Original Prints* (Polygon), *New Writing Scotland* and *Northern Lights* (Unwin Hyman).

HENRIETTA SOAMES was born in England of Hungarian-Czech parents. She has supported her writing with various jobs from selling horoscopes to washing up in wine bars. She now lives in London and her stories have been broadcast on Radio Four and appeared in *London Magazine*.

SUE SULLY was born in Yorkshire. She now lives in Somerset and her first novel, *The Unambitious Man*, was published in 1986. Her stories have appeared in magazines and have been broadcast on Radio Four's *Morning Story*. Her second novel, *The Barleyfield*, was published recently by William Heinemann.

JOHN TOWNSEND works with computers. He lives in Southport and has been writing for four years. His work has been featured in *Fiction Magazine*, *Panurge*, and *Stand*. He was fifth prize winner in the *Stand* 1987 Competition and won second prize in the 1989 Berkshire Literary Festival Competition.